Published
in conjunction with
THE MUSIC OF
PAUL BOWLES FESTIVAL
THE EOS ENSEMBLE
JONATHAN SHEFFER
CONDUCTOR
19-21 SEPTEMBER 1995
ALICE TULLY HALL
LINCOLN CENTER
NEW YORK

Edited by
Claudia SWAN

Eos Music Inc.

Jonathan SHEFFER
Artistic Director

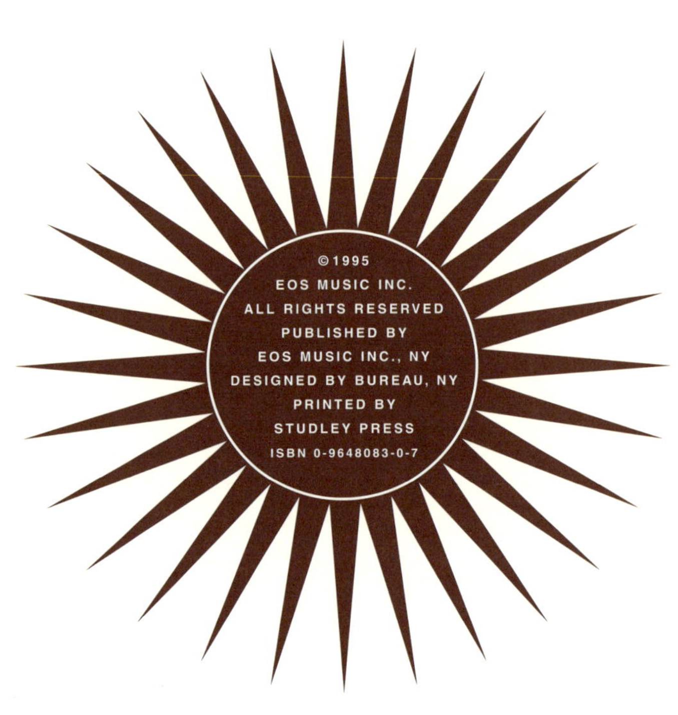
©1995
EOS MUSIC INC.
ALL RIGHTS RESERVED
PUBLISHED BY
EOS MUSIC INC., NY
DESIGNED BY BUREAU, NY
PRINTED BY
STUDLEY PRESS
ISBN 0-9648083-0-7

23/v/95

Dear Jonathan Sheffer:

I hope this note reaches you before you leave New York. It's merely to acknowledge receipt of the orchestrated suite of songs. It is certainly impressive, pristine, beautiful to behold, and very likely will sound the way I imagine it should.

My health varies from day to day. If I'm lucky, by the time you get here I'll be able to walk properly without fear of falling. Lacking that, I can always lie here quietly in bed.

I see that there is no mention of the texts of the songs, and I think there should be, somewhere. (One by Stein, two by Jane, and three by me.) Anyway, we shall have time to talk about details.

It will be a pleasure to see you. I regret that I shan't be able to assume the rôle of cicerone, but fortunately Phillip is here and can take over very satisfactorily. The drought has made life difficult. Water is brought in oil tankers from the south; the newspapers say it is "contaminated," but we drink bottled water in any case.

So, until very soon.

Best,

Paul Bowles

(Preface)

The Condition of Art

by
Jonathan Sheffer

This book is a collection of information, impressions and images that seek to describe and evoke the musical world of Paul Bowles. Its aim is to acquaint you with a writer who, like Boito and E.T.A. Hoffman before him, thought of himself as a composer before others thought of him as a writer.

Walter Pater's assertion that "all art constantly aspires towards the condition of music" seems to run aground in the case of Paul Bowles, a composer whose music constantly aspires towards the condition of art.

In his life, and particularly in his fiction, Bowles has found a certain equilibrium by placing himself and his characters at the very edge of a void. He grew up in New York, but his wanderings have taken him to the most remote parts of the globe. He has lived for nearly fifty years in the chaotic and alien culture of Morocco, worlds away from the sounds and energy of Times Square. It is hard to imagine the hot-house sensibility of Broadway surviving under the blistering sky of the Sahara. His journey seems to have been inward as well as outward: As he said to me recently, even before he quit America he was "tired" of composing for this play and that small commission, which is how he earned his living before the success of his first novel. Rather than pouring his foreign experiences back into the theater, he wrote books about the new worlds he had found.

The majority of Bowles' music has been unplayed for fifty years, unavailable to the public and unpromoted by the composer himself. I have been asked countless times, during the period I was preparing these concerts, what is his music like? The answer depends upon the circumstance: when speaking to musicians, I say, "It doesn't employ development, but favors a succession of short song-forms"; when speaking to record companies, I say, "It's jazzy, like weird Tin

Pan Alley." For the purposes of this book, I would add that it reflects the character of Bowles himself: jittery, mysterious, impatient, toying with discord and lacking hasty resolution. His life seems to me to have had a restlessness that seeks the borders of infinite spaces. Likewise, his music embellishes familiar sounds and forms with a grumpy curiosity and a relentless off-balance quality.

Paul Bowles' music employs a vividly specific vocabulary, leaving a narrow but incisive impression. His only formal training was a sort of apprenticeship to Aaron Copland. From an interpreter's standpoint, the music looks at times quite odd on the page, with harmonies misspelled, phrases of unusual length and curiously "laconic" expressive markings directing interpretation. Bowles has called his own compositional style "limited," and Virgil Thomson speculated that his shift into a literary career came at the point at which his training no longer served him. That, combined with a natural impatience, reflected in his expatriot existence, may explain the relative brevity of his exclusively musical career.

The "condition of art" I refer to is one of representation, as it defines the function of music that Bowles has assigned to his work. He accompanied scores of plays and art films, which often forced his composing into rigid constraints of "gesture" and form. He once wrote of "making music which would be expressive, and yet not in the oratorical way European art-music is expressive...replac[ing] what seemed to me the incredibly formal idiom of delivery taken for granted as the psychological basis for forming melodic logic." These ideas are everywhere in his music: his songs lightly outline the shape of their poetry, reserving precious little for passages of unsung music. His concerto and sonatas are collages — collisions, at times — of brief and stylish moods. I can think of no other composer whose musical ambitions have been so happily circumscribed, and yet so effective.

For those of you who seek to nurture the legacy of our country's music, and to take it to your hearts, I hope we have removed a critical levee of sorts, and helped a small stream flow back into the great main current to which it has been lost.

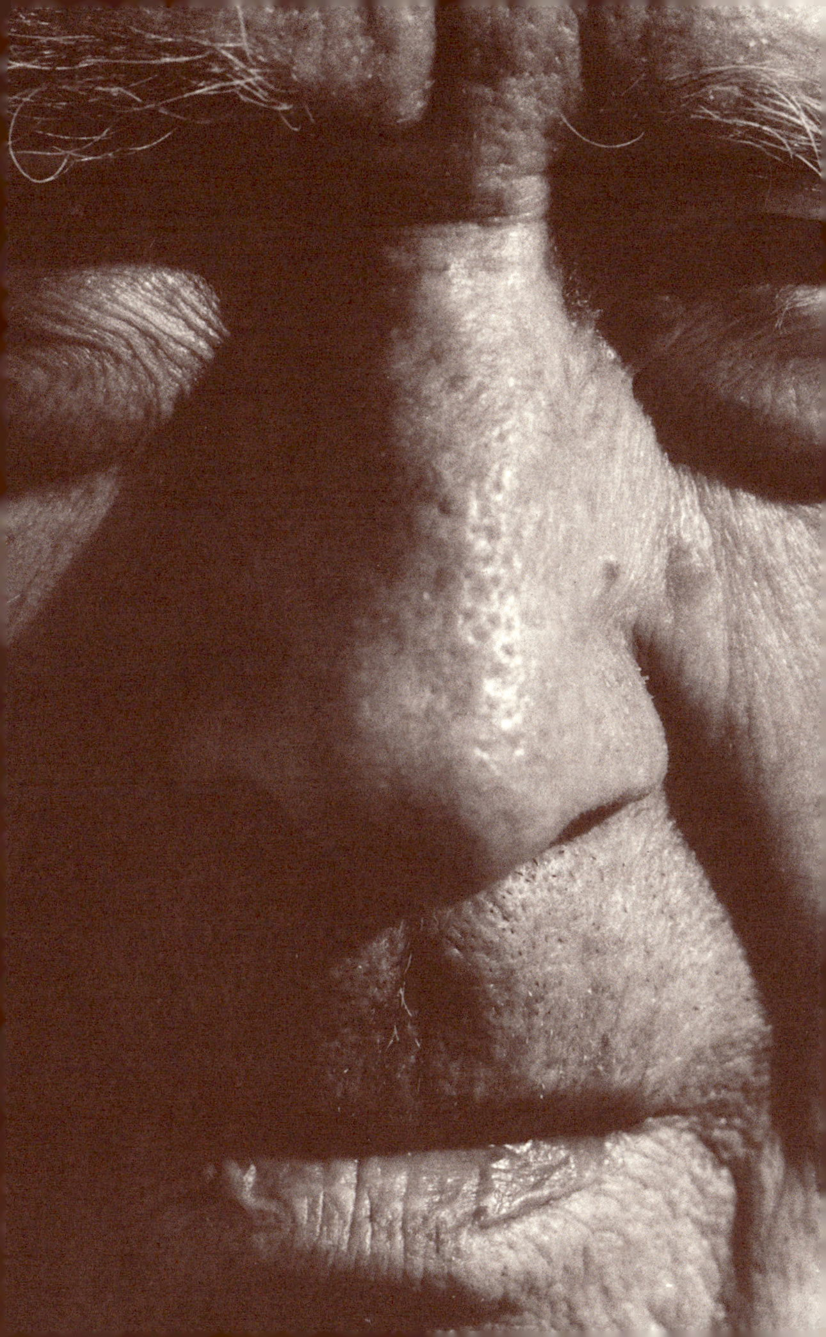

Bowles on Bowles (circa 1944)

The following biographical sketch, complete to circa 1944, was composed by Bowles himself, for inclusion in *American Composers Today. A Biographical and Critical Guide*, compiled and edited by David Ewen (New York, 1949).

p. 5

I was born in New York on 30 December 1910 and divided the first sixteen years of my life between that city and various country houses in New England and upper New York State. My first interest in music came from a purely hypnotic reaction that musical sounds always had on me—not music itself, for it always had formal patterns (even jazz), and showed direction, had some sort of climax and worst of all had a predictable end. I refer to the musical sounds I could produce myself by spinning a large musical top or by sliding a metal object up and down the strings of a German zither my grandfather had given me, or the creaking of a rusty door hinge; these sounds seemed to me the culmination of beauty, and always put me promptly into a non-thinking state which lasted as long as I repeated the sounds. I confess that these basic infantile criteria still seem perfectly valid to me, because they still operate on me with as much force as ever.

When I first heard Arabic music on records, I determined to go and live where I could be surrounded by sounds like those because there seemed very little else one could ask for in life. Accordingly, when I was twenty, I went to Morocco and started a four-year sojourn (with European interludes) in North Africa. The Sahara was a good place to write purely Occidental music, since one uses the music that is there simply for living, and not as material for anything else.

For a year and a half prior to going to North Africa, I had been having daily lessons with Aaron Copland, first in New York, and then in Berlin. In Paris, I used to take my things to Virgil Thomson, whose matter-of-fact attitude toward music at first seemed brutal to me, and then, when I had accepted it, the properly healthy one. From 1931 to 1934, I studied with Nadia Boulanger, Roger Sessions, and Israel Citkowitz. All this, however, should not be considered a formal musical education, as I never did have the patience to continue with my studies, and probably learned very little from them.

What interested me the most in the writing of music at that time was the possibility of making music which would be expressive, and yet not in the oratorical way European art-music is expressive. Conversational inflections, even the ones of imaginary conversational remarks inside the head, should replace what seemed to me the incredibly formal idiom of delivery taken for

GRANTED AS THE PSYCHOLOGICAL BASIS FOR FORMING MELODIC LOGIC. FROM THE POINT OF VIEW OF ESTABLISHING A CONNECTION WITH A PUBLIC, THIS DESIRE WAS PROBABLY DISASTROUS FOR ME; PEOPLE ARE NOT INTERESTED IN PSYCHOLOGICAL REALISM IN MUSIC. WHAT REALLY INTERESTS THEM IS A GOOD SHOW. WHICH, OF COURSE, INVOLVES USING THE TRADITIONAL MELODIC INFLECTIONS OF SPEECHIFYING, ALONG WITH ALL THE TRAPPINGS OF SOUND, FORMAL PATTERNS, AND EMOTIONAL DIRECTION THIS DEVICE WOULD LOGICALLY AND TECHNICALLY ENTAIL.

THEN I DISCOVERED THAT "INCIDENTAL MUSIC" FOR THE THEATER WAS ONE PERFECT MEDIUM FOR CARRYING OUT SOME OF THE IDEAS I HAD SUBCONSCIOUSLY BEEN TRYING TO EXPRESS. HERE IT IS NO LONGER A CRIME, BUT A VIRTUE, FOR A COMPOSER TO PRESCIND THE EMOTIONAL CONTENT OF HIS MUSIC BEFORE PRESENTING IT; HERE HE CAN SAY EXACTLY WHAT HE WANTS, AND EVERYONE WILL UNDERSTAND IT (ALTHOUGH, OF COURSE, NO ONE LISTENS TO IT BECAUSE THE SPOKEN WORD AND THE VISUAL ACTION TAKE PRECEDENCE IN THE EXERCISING OF THE SPECTATOR'S RECEPTIVE FACULTIES). HERE, AND IN WRITING FOR FILMS TOO, ONE CAN WITH IMMUNITY WRITE CLIMAXLESS MUSIC, HYPNOTIC MUSIC IN ONE OF THE EXACT SENSES OF THE WORD, IN THAT IT MAKES ITS EFFECT WITHOUT THE SPECTATOR'S BEING AWARE OF IT. FOR THE PAST FEW YEARS I HAVE BEEN PUTTING MUCH OF MY ENERGY INTO THE WRITING OF FUNCTIONAL SCORES, FOR THE THEATER *(My Heart's in the Highlands* [1939], *Twelfth Night* [1940], *Jacobowsky and the Colonel* [1944], *Watch on the Rhine* [1940/41], *The Glass Menagerie* [1944]*)*, FOR BALLETS, FOR THE FILMS. EACH YEAR, HOWEVER, HAS BEEN SPENT PARTLY IN SOME REGION OF LATIN AMERICA, WHERE THE MUSIC—AFTER THAT OF SPAIN, AFRICA, GREECE, AND THE LEVANT—SEEMS TO ME TO CONTAIN THE PHILOSOPHICAL AND EMOTIONAL ELEMENTS I NEED IN ORDER TO KEEP HAPPY.

"YOU DIDN'T WANT EVEN TO MEET PROKOFIEV?"

INTERVIEW BY PHILLIP RAMEY

PHILLIP RAMEY: WHEN DID YOU BEGIN TO COMPOSE?

PAUL BOWLES: I started as a small child, with songs. At one point I thought I was writing an opera. It was titled *Le Carré* and subtitled "an opera in nine chapters," so you can see how, even then, I got my arts mixed up. The plot concerned two men who decide to exchange wives. The setting was Stanley, in the Falkland Islands. This was just after the First World War and nobody had ever heard of the Falklands. Nor had I, except that I found them on a map.

PR: WHAT WAS YOUR EARLY TRAINING?

PB: I had two lessons a week, one in piano, the other in ear-training and theory. I wrote some small piano pieces at that time, when I was eight or nine. What I liked particularly was popular music, so I tried to write Broadway-like tunes. Of course they were no good. Nothing I composed then was any good. Naturally.

PR: HOW DID IT HAPPEN THAT YOU WERE ABLE TO STUDY WITH AARON COPLAND?

PB: Henry Cowell arranged that. I met Aaron in late 1929, when I was eighteen. Of course, I knew of him, because of the Copland-Sessions Concerts, but I had never heard a note of his music.

PR: YOU CAME TO ADMIRE HIM AS A COMPOSER?

PB: At that age I think that if one admires at all one admires wholeheartedly, and I did. He seemed to me the ideal of what a composer should be because he knew exactly why he put down every note.

PR: AARON ONCE TOLD ME THAT YOU WERE HARDLY AN EXEMPLARY STUDENT.

PB: True. He gave me figured basses to do every day, and we analyzed Mozart sonatas. I didn't enjoy any of it. Who would? It was no fun. Aaron used to shrug his shoulders and say, "If you don't work now when you're twenty, no one will love you when you're thirty." Aaron also called me "militantly non-professional." I love that word militant—I suppose he meant anti-academic, which I certainly was. But learning meant studying. (I did, however, compose my little *Sonata for Oboe and Clarinet* when I was with him in Morocco in 1931, but I didn't consider that to be work.) I thought that I could do what I wanted to do without any rigorous training.

PR: IS THAT WHY YOU REFUSED STUDIES WITH TWO IMPORTANT FIGURES OF TWENTIETH-CENTURY MUSIC, NADIA BOULANGER AND SERGEI PROKOFIEV?

PB: Of course. The key word there is study. It's a dirty word.

PR: DID YOU THINK THEY MIGHT BE TOO-STRICT TASKMASTERS?

PB: I could tell from Boulanger's personality that she would be strict. I had never met Prokofiev, but I had a Russian friend in Paris, Madame Daniloff, who knew him, and she said she would arrange for me to see him. I liked his music very much, especially a ballet I had seen performed by the Diaghilev company, *Pas d'Acier*, but the idea of meeting him frightened me. Nonetheless, Madame Daniloff made an appointment for three o'clock the following Monday. That day, after lunch, I found myself packing suitcases and taking a taxi to the Gare de l'Est. I bought a ticket to the farthest destination, which was Saverne in Alsace, and got on the train. I don't know what was the matter with me.

PR:
YOU DIDN'T WANT EVEN TO MEET PROKOFIEV?

PB: No, because if I had then he might have accepted me as a student. Later, we exchanged letters, and he wrote something like, "I am sorry that you were prevented from coming to see me last May, but I should like to warn you against the people you are seeing in America. Music is not headed in that direction." I had mentioned Copland to Prokofiev, and when I showed Aaron the letter he loved it. He laughed and laughed. I finally did meet Prokofiev in New York in 1936, just before he returned to Russia for good. At lunch he was serious and forbidding, and never smiled. Perhaps he was worried. I thought he was mad to go back.

PR:
MUSICALLY, YOU ARE A SELF-CONFESSED MINIATURIST, PRIMARILY A COMPOSER OF BRIEF, EPISODIC PIECES.

PB: For me, short, simple pieces were the most satisfying, perhaps because I didn't know how to appreciate long, complex ones. I wasn't certain how such pieces were made.

PR:
BUT DIDN'T YOU WANT TO FIND OUT? YOU WEREN'T STUPID.

PB: It was not a question of intelligence. I'm not complaining that I was dumb. I think that, largely, it was a matter of what Gertrude Stein called self-sufficiency.

PR: You never desired to create large-scale works—a symphony, for instance?

PB: No! I didn't think in those terms at all. My ideal was to write small pieces with only as many notes as absolutely necessary; pieces which could be listened to many times and would be fun to hear. I admit that's rather limiting. Formally, those pieces scarcely exist. As a composer, I think of myself as someone as marginal as Louis Moreau Gottschalk or Reynaldo Hahn.

PR: Is that part of your philosophy, that composing music and listening to it should be fun?

PB: Of course. What else is there in life but fun?

PR: Some composers of my acquaintance say that writing music is an agony.

PB (laughing): If *they* want agony, that's fine.

PR: What do you see as the function, if any, of concert music?

PB: First, I suppose, it has to entertain. When one hears the word entertainment, one thinks of show biz, but of course that isn't it. Music should engage the attention of the listener and make him more aware of what sound can do to him.

PR:

JUST THAT? YOU DON'T THINK THAT CONCERT MUSIC MIGHT HAVE, IN THE OLD TEUTONIC-ROMANTIC SENSE, SOME HIGH MORAL PURPOSE?

PB: None whatever. Good concert music expounds the philosophy of sound: where sounds come from and what they do.

PR:

BY CITING AN ENTERTAINMENT FACTOR, ARE YOU SUGGESTING POPULISM?

PB: No. I'm presupposing a sophisticated ear. The unsophisticated ear—the so-called man in the street—will probably not be in a concert hall.

PR:

DID YOU TAKE ANY PLEASURE IN THE ULTRA-SOPHISTICATED PROGRAMS THAT THE LEAGUE OF COMPOSERS GAVE IN NEW YORK IN THE 1930S AND '40S?

PB: Not unless they played a piece of mine, which was seldom. But, then, I think my music was more entertaining than the other things they were presenting, which tended to be by the academic crowd. By entertaining I mean easier to listen to. Those were highly specialized concerts. The general public never attended them.

PR:

THE MUSIC THEY PLAYED WAS DEADLY SERIOUS, WITH LITTLE CHARM?

PB: Yes, and there is no entertainment without charm.

PR:

BUT OTHERS MIGHT FIND, FOR INSTANCE, AN EARNEST BEETHOVEN QUARTET ENTERTAINING.

PB (laughing): You're not interviewing those others.

PR:
WHY DO YOU FIND BEETHOVEN'S MUSIC DISTASTEFUL?

PB: For one thing, because you have to wait so long for it to change.

PR:
IS IT TOO SERIOUS AND DETERMINED FOR YOU, NOT EPISODIC ENOUGH?

PB: Probably.

PR:
OF COURSE, GENERALLY SPEAKING, BEETHOVEN WAS UNINTERESTED IN CHARMING THE LISTENER. MORE IN IMPRESSING HIM.

PB: Ah, I was afraid of that!

PR:
YOU DON'T CARE FOR IMPRESSIVE, SELF-IMPORTANT MUSIC.

PB: How could I? In my own music I never liked to raise my voice. It was often more in the manner of an aside. That's partly why I prefer French music to German. The French were not striving to be impressive. It was something else they sought: exactitude of tone, starting with Couperin and continuing to Debussy, Ravel and Poulenc. The German aesthetic is foreign to me.

PR:
SO YOU HAVE NEVER ATTEMPTED TO WRITE ANY "SERIOUS," "IMPRESSIVE" MUSIC.

PB: It would embarrass me too much. I would be ashamed of it. It would be like writing prose that seeks to impress.

PR:
THEN YOUR MUSIC IS NOT MEANT TO BE TAKEN SERIOUSLY?

PB: I don't mind if other people take it seriously, but I don't. I certainly never intended it to be impressive. But, of course, you can take the lightest piano piece of Satie seriously.

PR: Although Copland had his lighter side, basically he was a serious composer. I know that you admire many of his works, especially the *Piano Variations*.

PB: Aaron was very serious, and most of his music is meant to be impressive. It expounds, often using rhetoric familiar from the nineteenth century, even from Beethoven. The *Piano Variations* is my favorite of all his serious concert music, and certainly its gestures are meant to impress the listener. But I admire the *Variations* for another reason: as I listen, I am aware of every detail of its construction; its beams and struts are beautifully visible, unmarred by any ornamentation. You cannot say that about "impressive" music by Germanic composers such as Gustav Mahler, Richard Strauss and Jan Sibelius.

PR: I knew you didn't like Mahler, but I didn't realize you felt strongly about Strauss and Sibelius.

PB: To my mind, Richard Strauss is a perfect example of what shouldn't be.

PR: I remember Copland saying that during the 1920s and '30s he considered Sibelius to be "the Enemy."

PB: As far as I'm concerned, you can have all seven of his symphonies, with my compliments.

PR: Sibelius is said to have composed an eighth symphony and then destroyed it.

PB: He finally caught on.

PR:

AM I RIGHT IN THINKING THAT IGOR STRAVINSKY IS YOUR FAVORITE COMPOSER?

PB: Yes, although I don't suppose I would put him ahead of Johann Sebastian Bach. But certainly ahead of anybody in the past two centuries.

PR:

I THINK IT'S EXTRAORDINARY THE WAY STRAVINSKY KEPT REINVENTING HIMSELF.

PB: So do I. When I was a kid, I liked the early Russian phase, especially *L'Oiseau de Feu*. But the later neo-classic works seem to me more solid and interesting, for instance, the *Concerto for Piano and Wind Instruments*—a great piece. I very much admire Stravinsky's intellect. I think he was brighter than other composers and you find that quality especially in the neo-classic scores. He had a wonderful gift for orchestration, perverse orchestration. He made the instruments sound as they hadn't sounded before, by using the "wrong" registers, by which I mean unusual registers. And his music was emotionally cool, which I appreciate.

PR:

AS A YOUNG MAN, WERE YOU BOWLED OVER BY *LE SACRE DU PRINTEMPS?*

PB: Of course. Like everyone else. Except that the first time I heard the music I had the misfortune to see it danced, by Martha Graham. If I'd just been listening to an orchestral performance I probably would have been even more bowled over by *Le Sacre*. But there was this visual thing on top of it that got in the way of enjoyment.

PR:

THE AWKWARD, EVEN GROTESQUE, GESTURES OF MARTHA GRAHAM.

PB: Which didn't necessarily come out of the music. Someone else could have made other gestures that might have been more in keeping with it.

PR:

WHAT ARE SOME OF YOUR OTHER FAVORITE STRAVINSKY WORKS?

PB: The Gluck-like, very end-of-the-eighteenth-century *Apollo*, which holds together beautifully from beginning to end. *Le Baiser de la Fée*—so very Tchaikovsky without being Tchaikovsky. *Les Noces*. The *Symphonies of Wind Instruments*, the *Symphony in C*, and the *Symphony in Three Movements*.

PR:

OEDIPUS REX?

PB: No, because I don't like vocal music. Also, it sounds to me like fake Stravinsky. And that old recording is so ridiculous, with Jean Cocteau coming in every few minutes, crying in French: "The terrible things that have happened to Thebes!"

PR:

HOW ABOUT THE LATE, SERIAL-INFLECTED PIECES, SUCH AS THE *REQUIEM CANTICLES*?

PB: No, no, no, no. I don't like his twelve-tone music. It's as though someone had rewritten some Schoenberg to sound like Stravinsky. It's Stravinsky-orchestrated, so you couldn't really mistake it. But even so, the material is so sad. Stravinsky went out of his way not to make the kind of music he would naturally make.

PR:

DID YOU EVER MEET HIM?

PB: Yes, once. In Symphony Hall, Boston, in what was probably Serge Koussevitzky's salon. He seemed very civilized, not eccentric in any way. We had tea, and he poured it for me from a teapot. I liked that.

I had a dream about Stravinsky last night. We were in the same hotel and I went to his room to see him because I wanted to hear certain of his pieces with which I was unfamiliar. He said, "It's all right, I have them on compact discs and will lend them to you, but just for a day." For some reason I had brought my parrot with me. It was screaming its head off and I kept yelling, "Shut up!" Stravinsky just smiled, a very ironic smile, as though he knew ahead of time how I would react to the music. He told me the titles of the pieces, but I had never heard of any of them. I carried the CDs down the hall in my right hand and the parrot's cage in my left. I didn't know where to put the parrot, but finally left it on the balcony, where it continued to scream so loudly that it was impossible to listen to the music. So I never heard anything, but Stravinsky did at least lend me the CDs.

PR: OF COURSE IN HIS DAY THERE WERE NO COMPACT DISCS.

PB: No. But it might just as well have been Mozart, agreeing to let me have his player-piano rolls.

PR: CONCERNING YOUR UNUSUAL DUAL CAREERS IN MUSIC AND PROSE: YOU ONCE MENTIONED THAT YOU THOUGHT THEY INVOLVED DIFFERENT PARTS OF THE BRAIN.

PB: Who knows how the mind is divided? I always found it a great relief to write if I had been composing; and if I had been writing it was wonderful to sit down and compose.

PR: WHY DO YOU SUPPOSE YOUR PROSE IS SO OFTEN "DARK," YOUR MUSIC LIGHT?

PB: Perhaps because I didn't know how to compose "dark" music.

PR: DID YOU EVER TRY?

PB: Once—in 1931, in Berlin. It was a piano piece, now lost, called *Tamanar,* named after a place down in southern

Morocco where the High Atlas mountains fall into the Atlantic Ocean. The music was loud and sinister, by which I mean the harmony was sinister—dissonant and heavy. When I worked at it, people would begin screaming, *"Fenster zu!"* (Shut the window!) across the courtyard, threatening to call the police. They didn't want to hear such a racket.

PR: ULTIMATELY, YOUR SERIOUS SIDE CAME OUT IN YOUR BOOKS.

PB: Certainly not in my musical compositions. Lenny Bernstein always said that my music sounded post-coital.

PR: YOUR FICTION IS FULL OF HORRIFIC INCIDENTS THAT MIGHT, IN A SENSE, BE CONSIDERED GESTURAL. THEY CATCH THE READER'S ATTENTION SOMEWHAT IN THE WAY MUSICAL GESTURES CATCH THE LISTENER'S.

PB: But I don't think that's so shameful in prose because it's connected with the meaning of the story.

PR: COPLAND ONCE TOLD ME THAT YOU WROTE "ENGAGING MUSIC THAT HAD ITS OWN STYLE, THOUGH IT WASN'T DEMANDINGLY *MODERNE*." HE ALSO SAID, "I'VE NEVER KNOWN PAUL TO WRITE A DULL PIECE."

PB: I don't object to that. Would you? Though my music certainly wasn't trying to be "modern," and Aaron never suggested that I write dissonant music. He would point out my failings, but apparently they were technical rather than stylistic.

PR: Do you compose sequentially, from beginning to end?

PB: Always.

PR: Copland often did not work that way. He would compose bits and pieces of a movement and eventually fit them together so that everything was coherent.

PB: That wouldn't work for me. That's a synthetic way I couldn't manage.

PR: In that sense, Copland's approach to composition was more intellectual than yours.

PB: It would have to be.

PR: I know you seldom revise your prose, for you are intent on getting things right the first time. But did you make major revisions in your musical scores?

PB: No. I would have lost everything if I had.

PR: How much influence has jazz had on your music?

PB: A lot of Copland is strictly out of jazz, but I never used it. Even if one loves jazz, it is very difficult to have anything to do with it. By jazz, you mean American Black music. As a composer, I was always careful to stay away from it because I wasn't black and, thus, wouldn't have been able to get the exact effect.

PR:

ALTHOUGH YOU HAVE WRITTEN A GREAT MANY SONGS, I SUSPECT THAT YOUR REAL FORTE IS INSTRUMENTAL MUSIC.

PB: That's true, because instrumental music is not so damned *human*. When I listen to music I don't want to be reminded of human beings all the time, and when someone is singing you can't help but be. You have a mental image of either a man or a woman with an open mouth, and it's not pleasant. I hate most vocal Western art music, although I don't mind choral music. I do not like listening to art songs.

PR:

DOES IT STRIKE YOU AS UNNATURAL TO SEE SOMEONE STANDING BY A PIANO EMOTING AND AGONIZING?

PB: Of course. Singers spend years learning to be unnatural. *Bel canto!* It's a horrible noise, like a bull bellowing. The way Asian singers sound is much more natural and satisfying—more like instruments. However, Gregorian chant is beautiful. I don't find a group of people singing so objectionable, even in harmonization, which is not so good as in unison. That is certainly better than a soprano or a tenor singing solo.

PR:

YET THE PUBLISHED COLLECTION OF YOUR SOLO SONGS IS NEARLY AN INCH THICK.

PB: That's fewer than half of them.

PR:

YOUR ACTIVITY IN THIS AREA MUST HAVE TO DO WITH TEXTS.

PB: Obviously I had an itch to set words to music.

PR:

TEXTS, OF COURSE, ADD ANOTHER HUMAN ELEMENT.

PB: That can be annoying. It's nice if the text is in Hungarian, then you don't have to bother trying to find out what is being said. If it's in English, you just get a word here and there anyway. If it's in French, it's part of the ambience. If it's in German, you can always get out fast! I like Bartók's opera, *Bluebeard's Castle*. I don't know what is being sung, but at least the words don't interfere with the music.

PR:

DESPITE YOUR DISLIKE OF SONGS IN GENERAL, DO YOU ENJOY HEARING YOUR OWN?

PB: If the performer is really good and *simpático*. Then, sometimes I think: yes, that's the kind of singing I was hoping for. To me, the best singers are simply immersed in the music. They are not saying, "*I* am singing this."

PR:

YOU WOULDN'T CARE FOR AN OPERATIC VOICE.

PB: No, because most of my songs are only lyrical. It goes without saying that singers ought to have decent voices, but they seldom do.

PR:

WHICH SINGERS WHO HAVE PERFORMED YOUR SONGS HAVE YOU LIKED?

PB: Few. Jennie Tourel. Romolo de Spirito. Libby Holman. Nina Tarasova. Donald Gramm. More recently, William Sharp.

PR:

DURING THE 1930S AND '40S, WHEN YOU LIVED IN NEW YORK, YOU PRODUCED A CONSIDERABLE AMOUNT OF *GEBRAUCHSMUSIK*—SCORES FOR THE THEATER AND FOR FILMS.

PB: I made my living doing that. It was satisfying because I was able to hear the music almost immediately, to see what it did and how it fulfilled its function.

PR:

AND THERE WERE NO PROBLEMS OF EXTENDED FORM.

PB: Right.

PR:

BEFORE THE COMMISSIONS FOR FUNCTIONAL MUSIC, YOU WERE COMPOSING SOLELY FOR YOURSELF—FOR INSTANCE, THE EARLY PIANO PIECES AND SONGS, THE *FLUTE SONATA*, *VIOLIN SONATA*, *SONATA FOR OBOE AND CLARINET*, THE *SCÈNES D'ANABASE* FOR TENOR, OBOE AND PIANO, THE *SUITE FOR SMALL ORCHESTRA*?

PB: Yes. I thought that was natural. Nothing was commissioned until 1936, when Virgil Thomson arranged for me to do the score for the John Houseman and Orson Welles production *Horse Eats Hat*. I was enthusiastic because it was a marvelous play, a clever adaptation of a farce by Eugène Labiche. Virgil gave me a good deal of help with the orchestration, which was for chamber orchestra, because I was an inexperienced orchestrator and the music had to be done very quickly. He did most of the *tutti*s and I concentrated on sections which didn't require more than five or six instruments. For the second theater commission, *The Tragical History of Doctor Faustus*, Orson asked me directly and I did it alone. Virgil was in Paris at the time, and when he came back and looked at the billboard he said, "I see you got your name on the front of the theater all by yourself this time!"

PR:

WAS HE MIFFED?

PB: A little, I think. He didn't *say* he was, but the fact that he mentioned it indicated that.

PR:

LET'S TALK ABOUT SOME OF THE PIECES BEING PLAYED AT THE 1995 PAUL BOWLES MUSIC FESTIVAL, PRESENTED IN NEW YORK BY THE EOS ENSEMBLE. FIRST, *NOONDAY (MEDIODÍA)*, WRITTEN IN 1937.

PB: It's a suite of Mexican dances with restricted instrumentation— flute, clarinet, bassoon trumpet, 2 percussion, piano and strings. The three parts are "The Snake" (*La Culebra*), "The Dust" (*El Polvo*), and "The Sun" *(El Sol)*. The third dance was originally a piano piece, *Huapango No. 2*; it is strictly rhythmical—persistent, with the same pattern throughout. The first and, as far as I know, only performance of *Noonday* was given in February 1938, on the roof of the St. Regis Hotel in New York. I played the drums.

PR:

THE DOUBLE PIANO CONCERTO OF 1946 WAS WRITTEN FOR THE DUO-PIANISTS ARTHUR GOLD AND ROBERT FIZDALE. WAS THAT A COMMISSION?

PB: Yes, the second I had from them, the first being for the *Sonata for Two Pianos* of 1945. The commission specified two pianos with a small instrumental ensemble, something they could perform in New York at Town Hall.

PR:

THE CONCERTO IS YOUR MOST EXTENDED INSTRUMENTAL WORK.

PB: Yes. The *Picnic Cantata* (also a Gold and Fizdale commission) lasts longer, but it is more episodic, eight separate pieces with singers, whereas the Concerto has only four movements. I especially like the second, the scherzo, which is just for two pianos and percussion. I wrote some of that material way back when I was sixteen.

PR:

HOW DID THE ORCHESTRAL VERSION COME ABOUT?

PB: Gold and Fizdale wrote me that they had been approached by the Brussels Philharmonic, and that they thought it a good idea for me to make an arrangement of the Concerto for full orchestra. It took quite a while; I started it in 1947, on the ship coming to Tangier from New York, continued it in Fez, and eventually finished it in 1949. The new version was premiered in Brussels, but I was unable to go and have forgotten the date. I must say, the orchestration was a job. The parts had to be extracted, of course, and at the time the place to have that done was East Germany. But the copyists there were violently against the music, saying it was fascist. You know how the Comrades feel: no sense of humor. Some of them refused to have anything to do with the Concerto.

PR:

WHY WOULD COMMUNIST COPYISTS HAVE VIEWED YOUR EBULLIENT AND MELODIC PIECE THAT WAY?

PB: Because, I suppose, it was their idea that all music should sound like Anton von Webern.

PR:

I ASSUME THAT YOUR *SUITE FOR SMALL ORCHESTRA*, DATING AS IT DOES FROM 1932-33, WAS UNCOMMISSIONED.

PB: Yes. I wrote it for my own pleasure. There are three movements: *Pastorale*, *Havanaise* and *Divertissement*. The *Pastorale* is made up of simple and repetitious North African melodies that I remembered from a trip to Algeria in 1933. It's lyrical and very brief.

PR:

DO THOSE MELODIES SOUND EXOTIC TO OCCIDENTAL EARS?

PB: I would think so. I used exactly the same melodies in my incidental music to *Salomé*, which was written two years ago for synthesizer, for one of Joseph McPhillips' productions at the American School of Tangier.

PR:

AND THE *HAVANAISE* AND *DIVERTISSEMENT*?

PB: I remember composing the *Havanaise* in Agadir, in 1932. It's the longest of the three pieces, really a tango. The *Divertissement* is a fast piece. There is one melody that is obviously in Latin American (but not Mexican) style. I recall what Elliott Carter, at his meanest, wrote: "Bowles' procedure is to take folk tunes and deprive them of their meaning." But I never used Latin folk tunes; rather, I invented melodies in the manner of Latin folk music. When you do that, people think you've cribbed the tunes. Of *course* they are deprived of meaning, because they never had that meaning in the first place.

PR:

THE GLASS MENAGERIE SCORE WAS THE FIRST OF YOUR FOUR THEATRICAL COLLABORATIONS WITH TENNESSEE WILLIAMS.

PB: It was premiered in New York at the Playhouse on 31 March 1945, after a tryout in Chicago the previous December. I had to compose the entire score in one weekend. The problem was that the producer wouldn't give me a contract. He said he didn't think music needed to be paid for. Naturally I disagreed. Finally, on Friday evening, my agent got a lousy contract drawn up—for, I think, only fifty dollars. The music had to be ready by Monday.

PR:

What was the genesis of *The Wind Remains*?

PB: In 1941, I had a Guggenheim grant to write an opera. I was in Mexico at the time, and I didn't have a subject. But I had been corresponding with William Saroyan, for whose play *Love's Old Sweet Song* I had composed the music the year before. He said he would write a libretto, and he did. It was called *Opera! Opera!*, and I couldn't make any sense of it. About as sensible as the least sensible Gertrude Stein. I suppose he was confusing me with Virgil Thomson, and maybe Virgil could have used it but I didn't know what to do with it. So I turned to Federico García Lorca, whom I was always busy reading, and I came upon his Surrealist play *Así que Pasen Cinco Años* (which translates, "In Another Five Years or So") and thought several excerpts from that would make a good libretto. I began the music in Mexico and finished it in New York in late 1942.

PR:

Where did you get your title?

PB: From the end of the play, where the clown says: "The wind remains, and the sound of my violin." Instead of a violin, I used a wind machine, which I myself ran when the work was given at the Museum of Modern Art in New York, on 30 March 1943. Leonard Bernstein conducted, the choreography was by Merce Cunningham, and the sets by Oliver Smith. The two singers were Romolo de Spirito, tenor, and Jeanne Stephens, soprano. I remember that the hall had no proscenium and that poor Lenny did not seem happy having to conduct the orchestra—which was positioned onstage amidst the set—from the back wall of the stage where he was invisible to the audience, but he bore it bravely. Although there was a subsequent performance and recording (slightly abridged) of a concert version of *The Wind Remains* in 1956 (both arranged by my friend the composer Peggy Glanville-Hicks), the work has never again been staged. The trouble with *The Wind Remains* as an opera is that its text means nothing and goes nowhere. Of course, it isn't actually an opera, but rather a *zarzuela* consisting of solo songs, spoken dialogue, various instrumental sections, dances, and choruses. It lasts about half an hour.

PR: AFTER YOU SWITCHED TO PROSE AND RELOCATED YOURSELF IN MOROCCO IN 1947, YOUR MUSIC, ESPECIALLY THE CONCERT MUSIC, WAS LARGELY FORGOTTEN. HOW DO YOU FEEL ABOUT THE PRESENT REVIVAL OF INTEREST—THE VARIOUS CONCERTS AND NEW RECORDINGS?

PB: It's flattering—ego massage. I see my music as part of the past. I'm curious to know how it holds up, but in the context of 1935, not 1995.

PR: AREN'T YOU CURIOUS ABOUT HOW AUDIENCES RESPOND TO IT TODAY?

PB: I suppose the best they could think about it is that it has charm. That's already saying a lot.

JUNE 1995 TANGIER

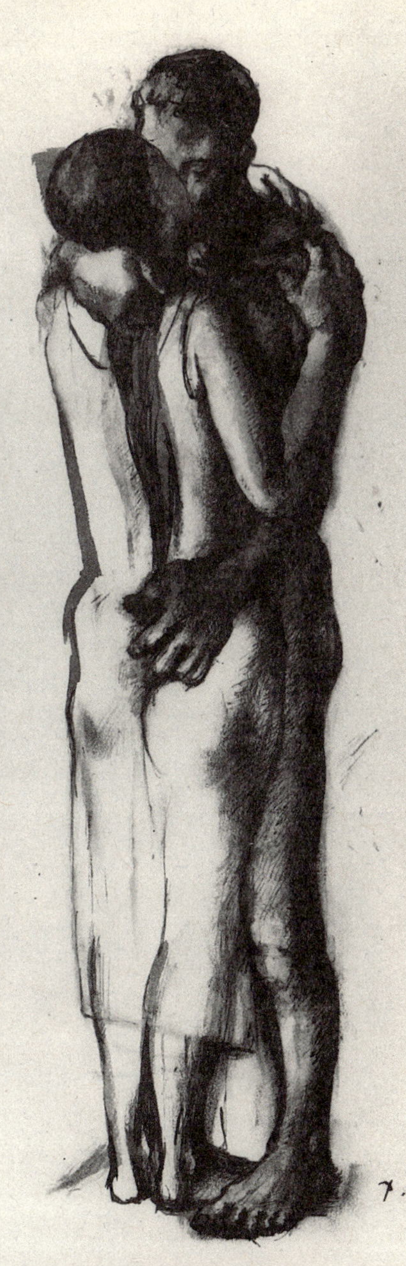

On Hearing Bowles

by Eli Gottlieb

THE SLIMNESS, the leonine head of hair, the French-cut suits and taut-boned face — Paul Bowles, in photos, *looks* the writer more compellingly than any American has since Ezra Pound. He is Central Casting's dream of the artist, a steely bohemian who makes his way in the world through sheer force of will, tailoring and talent.

The truth isn't all that far away.

By the time of his emergence in the artistic scene of the late 1930s and early '40s, Bowles, a secretive child from that surpassingly strange locale called Long Island, New York, had reinvented himself from the ground up. Several years in Paris, Germany, Spain and North Africa had considerably broadened his cultural base, and with his new wife Jane at his side, the intriguingly *louche*, splendidly dressed composer became half of one of the most "in" couples in circulation, a *salon à deux* that travelled the world on zephyrs of alcohol and conversation, and during its time in New York associated with the best expatriate and American artists around, including W.H. Auden, Tennessee Williams, Leonard Bernstein, John Cage, and the eternally helpful Truman Capote.

By all accounts the Bowleses, though unconventional in their living arrangements, were entirely orthodox in their love and attachment to one another. She was quirky, abrupt, and performative by nature, while Bowles, as ever, tended towards watchful reserve. Interestingly enough, these same qualities carry over intact in their writing. Going from the prose of wife to husband is like stepping directly out of a busy intersection into the Sahara at noon. The work of Jane Bowles is invaded by precariousness at every level, with words that seem to flit and quiver within their sentences, shifting as if searching for a stable base. Paul Bowles' writing, by comparison, is as clean as a horizon-line. Fittingly for a man who has had the rare distinction of moving with equal ease in the worlds of literature and music, his written work is distinguished, overall, by the acuity of its tone. The narrating register is elastic and imperturbable at the same time, with a dryness produced not by lack of passion but by supreme self-control. Throughout the written *oeuvre*, from the suavely drawn violence of the early stories, into the symphonic richness of *The Sheltering Sky* and other novels, through the translations and travel writing, the poems, the correspondence and the late masterpiece *Points in Time*, there is everywhere evident a natural governance of the extremes of feeling, an exquisite sense of modulation and proportion.

That's why the surprise, when it happens, hits so hard—and there is nearly always a surprise in the fiction of Paul Bowles. The perfectly planed surfaces of the narratives inevitably carry a focused punch to the reader's vitals. Beneath the brooding landscapes and pitch-perfect dialogue, a heart of darkness beats, throbbing steadily through the misunderstandings that arise so often in Bowles' works between the linear Cartesians of the West and the multiform denizens of the "non-Christian world."

Bowles himself has complained of being typed unfairly as a writer of lurid dénouments, and has pointed to the many stories that deal with things no more frightening than disagreements between metropolitan couples, family reminiscences of Christmas, or, in one case, tender friendship between an elderly Swiss woman and a young Arab boy. But even in these apparently calmer treatments there is still a feeling of supervening menace, of the world subtly disarranged, of the established settings of life giving way, abruptly, to a backdrop charged with threat and chaos.

In addition to unwavering control of tone in his fiction, one should mention clarity and sharpness of expressive means. Bowles has said that he renounced composing music full-time because "there were a great many things I wanted to say that were too precise to express in musical terms."[1] The precision of his diction is in fact central to his achievement as a literary artist, and in his best work, the knife-edge joinery of the sentences is as fine as anything in our literature. Ernest Hemingway and Gertrude Stein harnessed some of the same white space around language, subverting the calm placement of letters on a page and revealing the river of jittery conditionality flowing beneath language; Albert Camus, in the famed "white style" of *The Stranger*, provided a new lesson in the ambient chill of syntax. Writers like Graham Greene drew sublimely savage portraits of Empire in decline. And yet none of them provided us with quite the same mix of dead-

1. *Conversations with Paul Bowles*, ed. Gena Dagel Caponi (Jackson, 1993), p.4.

panned understatement and ferocity of depiction, or staked as deep a claim on the worlds of drugs, "the primitive," altered states of consciousness, magic and incest as did Bowles. He is our very first home-grown existentialist, a man defiantly indifferent to the dictates of "literature" who has ended up creating a new branch of it entirely his own.

Perhaps for this reason, literary critics admit to extreme confusion in trying to pigeonhole his work. Certainly, they agree, he is a master of the "exotic." He is a superb moralist and cultural diagnostician, with a 19th-century Romantic view of the truth-telling powers of Nature. As for influences, there is the Gothicism of Edgar Allen Poe, clearly, and a leavening of André Gide. In psychological terms, Bowles' work expresses the divided self of R.D. Laing and is filled with the archetypal symbols of Carl Jung. But what is his writing "about"?

The question—finally unanswerable—leads us quite naturally to his music, which has the advantage, over writing, of being far more "about" itself. In listening to his work, one is immediately struck by the *freedom* of the music. Where the prose is always necessarily harnessed to the low gear of narrative, the lightsome inventions of his compositions surprise. There is a delicacy that one might have expected from the crystalline quality of his prose fiction, but nothing could have prepared one for the fluidity and ranging, aerial feeling of his music.

On a more thematic level, even a musical amateur can identify the recurrence of "native" musics in the compositions of Bowles. Throughout his work, both written and composed, Bowles has been a fierce champion of the indigenous. Interestingly, when music is vernacular it employs pre-existing motifs to make its point (essences of popular music, Mexican folksong, or Moroccan religious music are used and expected to be recognized as such). When fiction concentrates on the indigenous and local, though its aspirations may be similar, the writer necessarily uses *his* language rather than an already shaped motif, a situation that puts him at a double remove from the subject matter, and places him, accordingly, in double danger of condescension in his depictions. Amazingly, Bowles avoided these difficulties, found a way to retrieve and frame the living cultural stuffs of a variety of disappearing societies, and managed to do so in two different media which, it is increasingly clear, have very little directly to do with each other.

"THERE ARE THOSE WHO REFUSE TO SEE IN BOWLES ANYTHING MORE THAN A DILETTANTE"

AARON COPLAND AND PAUL BOWLES, CIRCA 1931

BY K. ROBERT SCHWARZ

Throughout his career as a composer, Paul Bowles has remained a proud auto-didact, projecting what Aaron Copland described as "a militantly non-professional air in relation to all music, including his own."[1] Although the literature on Bowles is filled with references to lessons he supposedly took with teachers as diverse as Copland, Nadia Boulanger, Roger Sessions, Virgil Thomson and Vittorio Rieti, it was only with Copland that Bowles came close to following a coherent course of study. Their relationship—initially that of mentor and protégé, later that of professional colleagues—continued until Copland's death in 1990. As late as 1984, Bowles sent Copland a newly-composed song as a birthday present, a setting of Tennessee Williams' *My Love Was Light*. Even today, Bowles continues to speak of Copland with a mixture of admiration and affection.

(1)
Aaron Copland, "America's Young Men—Ten Years Later," *Modern Music* XIII/4 (May-June 1936); reprinted in Aaron Copland, *Copland on Music* (Garden City, 1960), p. 162.

Despite their long association, Bowles actually studied with Copland only from 1929 through 1931. These were pivotal years in Bowles' compositional career: his earliest extant work, the *Sonata for Oboe and Clarinet* (1931), was written under Copland's tutelage; his first visit to Morocco was made with Copland at his side; and the first public performances of his music occurred at Copland's behest. No young composer had a better champion than Bowles found in Copland. And no older composer had a more obstreperous student than Copland found in Bowles.

"Copland had tried in New York teaching him harmony but had found him a stubborn pupil," Virgil Thomson recalled in his autobiography.[2] Recently, Bowles objected to the

(2)
Virgil Thomson, *Virgil Thomson* (New York, 1966), p. 206.

word "stubborn," but admitted that he had been opinionated. "I certainly expressed my silly taste. I had no right to have taste at that age. In order to have your tastes mean anything, you must know something. And I was extremely ignorant. All I did was know what I liked, which was absurd." [3]

(3) Interview of Paul Bowles by K. Robert Schwarz (hereinafter KRS), 13 July 1993.

Bowles first came into contact with Copland on 30 December 1928, when he attended one of the Copland-Sessions concerts of contemporary music in New York. "Because I had heard Copland's music ridiculed by several older people whose taste seemed antiquated, I assumed automatically that he was the most important composer in the United States," Bowles wrote in *Without Stopping*. (*WS*:98-99)* His estimation was correct. In the late 1920s and early '30s, Copland was the rising star among young American composers. After studying in Paris with Nadia Boulanger from 1921 to 1924, Copland had returned to the States determined to craft a recognizably American variety of modernism. Initially, he attempted a synthesis of jazz and concert music, as in *Music for the Theatre* (1925) and the *Piano Concerto* (1926). Later, he would craft a lean, dissonant, and pungently strident idiom that found its most powerful expression in the *Piano Variations* (1930) and the *Short Symphony* (1933).

p. 36

* REFERENCES TO Paul Bowles, *Without Stopping* (NEW YORK, 1972) ARE CITED WITHIN THE BODY OF THE TEXT AS (*WS*).

It was not until the winter of 1929 that Bowles and Copland finally met. Bowles had gone to visit Henry Cowell, and had shown the ardent experimentalist some of his music. Cowell apparently found it insufficiently radical, for he gave Bowles an amusingly snide letter to take to Copland: "Dear Aaron: This will introduce Paul Bowles. His music is very French, but it might interest you." (*WS*:98)

(4) Gena Dagel Caponi, *Paul Bowles: Romantic Savage* (Carbondale, 1994), p. 42.

Bowles immediately went to see Copland, who sensed that the young man was "born to be a composer," [4] but stressed that he did not give formal lessons. "He said, 'You know, I don't teach,' " Bowles recalled. "But from the letter of Cowell I think he understood I was looking for a mentor. So he said, 'Well, you can come mornings if you want for an hour, and we'll go over your music.' So I did. I think I went every day or every two days." [5]

(5) KRS, 12-13 July 1993.

This routine didn't last long, for Bowles had to return to the University of Virginia in Charlottesville for the spring semester of 1930. Since he couldn't be with Copland, he arranged for Copland to visit him. Copland, who arrived in April 1930, even performed part of his *Piano Concerto* before a hostile and ill-informed audience. "I think most of the people thought he was out of his mind," Bowles recalled. "I tried to drum up some trade, to get everybody who might possibly be interested to come and hear him. I'm now surprised that he agreed to play, because he was playing for a bunch of know-nothing provincials." [6]

(6) KRS, 12 July 1993.

Regular lessons didn't resume until late in the summer of 1930, when Bowles joined Copland at Yaddo, the artists' retreat in Saratoga Springs, New York, where Copland was working on the *Piano Variations*. At the very end of the season, Copland and Bowles drove to Vermont, where they visited Carl Ruggles, and to Massachussets, where they spent an afternoon with Sessions. Back in New York during the fall and winter of 1930-31, Bowles had a lesson with Copland nearly every day.

Copland's method was simple but sensible: to teach Bowles composition by using Mozart as a model. In order to learn harmonic analysis, Bowles had to work backwards and construct a figured bass from a Mozart piano sonata. He also had to play the sonata. "It had nothing to do with my pianistic skill or lack of it; he wasn't interested in that," Bowles recalled. "He was interested in the construction of the music. We got to a certain place and he would say, 'Now begins the development.' One could see that anyway, but he just made sure. I think we went on and on through all the Mozart piano sonatas. And we continued the same work in Berlin and again here [in Tangier]."

Valiantly, Copland attempted to teach some abstract principles of harmony and counterpoint to his reluctant pupil. "He gave me rules," Bowles said, laughing at the thought. "I don't remember what they were. Probably [forbidding] consecutive fifths, you know. He wasn't trying to teach; he was trying to show me. I wasn't aware of taking lessons, really. I was aware of being with Aaron Copland, much more than talking about a Mozart sonata. I think he was a great teacher. He made you look for things, which was better than having them thrust upon you." [7]

(7)
KRS, 13 July 1993.

In the spring of 1931, Copland was scheduled to go to Berlin, and it was decided that Bowles would join him. By April they were settled in Berlin, where they lunched regularly with Christopher Isherwood and Stephen Spender and attended opera performances. Bowles continued to have daily lessons with Copland, but worked on his own compositions only fitfully. "Music is so difficult," he wrote from Berlin to Edouard Roditi on 9 June. "One follows on the heels ten years behind of Antheil, Copland, Blitzstein, twenty years behind Hindemith, thirty behind Stravinsky." [8]

p. 38 Mostly, however, he was simply unmotivated. In July, he wrote to his college friend Bruce Morrissette that "i fear i am merely lazy. nothing can induce me to start on the chorales i must do before august first." [9] Apparently, Copland, who was now in Oxford, had left him with the sort of assignment appropriate to any young music student—the harmonizing of Bach chorales—and Bowles could not bear the thought of beginning it. In a letter to Roditi, Bowles admitted how little he had accomplished in Berlin: "i write not so often now, as i am working on mozart, and am trying to finish my sonata [for oboe and

(8)
Paul Bowles to Edouard Roditi, 9 June 1931, *In Touch: The Letters of Paul Bowles*, ed. Jeffrey Miller (New York, 1994) (hereinafter *IT*), p. 67.

(9)
Paul Bowles to Bruce Morrissette, July 1931, *IT*, p. 74. The absence of capitalization is a common trait of Bowles' letters during this period.

clarinet], which i have been doing since last autumn, and of which i have completed but one movement...ah well."[10]

(10)
Paul Bowles to Edouard Roditi, June or July 1931, *IT*, p. 73.

In the middle of July 1931, Bowles travelled to Bilignin, a village in the French Alps where Gertrude Stein and Alice B. Toklas had a summer house. Copland joined Bowles at the end of the month, and their plan was to proceed the following week to Nice, where they intended to rent a house on the Riviera. Stein promptly cross-examined Copland not only about Bowles' gifts as a composer, but about his seeming lack of motivation. In *The Autobiography of Alice B. Toklas*, Stein wrote that "it pleased her that Copeland [sic] said threateningly to him..., if you do not work now when you are twenty, when you are thirty, nobody will love you."[11] It was a remark that would haunt Bowles for years to come.

(11)
Gertrude Stein, *The Autobiography of Alice B. Toklas*, in *Selected Writings of Gertrude Stein*, ed. Carl Van Vechten (New York, 1972), pp. 236-7.

Stein got wind of the fact that Copland and Bowles were
heading to the Riviera, and was appalled. Morocco would be a much p. 39
better destination, she felt, and, as Copland recalled, "she quite literally talked us into changing our plans, and instead of the Riviera, we headed for Tangier."[12]

(12)
Aaron Copland and Vivian Perlis, *Copland: 1900 Through 1942* (New York, 1984), p. 188.

It was on " The Mountain," a ridge several kilometers outside of Tangier, that Bowles found a house to rent for the summer. A large villa reached by a dirt road, it was perched near cliffs that commanded an unobstructed view of Spain. "Aaron hesitated because the house was big, run-down, unfurnished, and isolated," Bowles wrote. "However, we decided to take it and immediately began buying the necessary beds, tables, chairs, and cooking equipment." (*WS*:127)

What was not so easy to procure was a piano, but since both Copland and Bowles composed at the keyboard, it was a necessity. Soon they rented a battered black upright, which arrived at their doorstep strapped to a donkey's back. When the donkey balked, the piano tumbled to the ground, and the instrument—once safely installed in the villa—was now desperately in need of tuning. Eventually the piano store sent a technician who "had no idea how to tune a piano and no sense of pitch." (*WS*:128)

The next morning, Copland went to work on his *Short Symphony* and Bowles returned to his *Sonata for Oboe and Clarinet*, but Copland was unable to concentrate. Bowles, typically, was far from unhappy to be distracted from his work. He delighted in the music that came from a distant part of the mountain, particularly the complex drum rhythms that continued for hours at a time. These did not amuse Copland. "That worries Aaron," Bowles wrote to Stein, "as he cannot get it out of his head that the Arabs are grieved about something, and are all set to go on the warpath."[13]

(13)
Paul Bowles to Gertrude Stein, August 1931, *IT*, p. 85.

Although the piano was still out of tune, Copland succeeded in creating some semblance of a daily routine. "Immediately after breakfast each morning Aaron gave me my harmony lesson; it included correcting the figured basses I had
p.40 prepared the day before," Bowles wrote. "I was still in the process of analyzing the Mozart piano sonatas. I worked lying in a deck chair in the lower garden, where I would not hear Aaron's chordal laboratory. Afternoons Aaron, who drank wine at lunch, took a nap upstairs, while I worked at the piano." (*WS*:129) In the evenings they would go into Tangier, to one of the Grand Socco cafes, and linger over dinner.

More recently, Bowles remembered this process as running a bit less smoothly. "He had the use of the piano at whatever hour he wanted. And I had the use of it when he didn't want it. I don't know why my music didn't disturb him. It didn't seem to. And obviously his didn't disturb me, because I heard it from the garden. I loved hearing him work on the *Short Symphony*."

The relationship between Copland and Bowles frequently grew tense. "He scolded me a lot," Bowles recalled. "He would say, 'Why didn't you do the work I gave you yesterday? Go and do it!' I would sulk. It became a very personal relationship. He wanted me to learn as much as possible from having been with him. But he wanted me to learn it in musical terms. And I learned a great deal from him in literary terms and in other ways."[14]

(14)
KRS, 13 July 1993.

As the summer of 1931 passed, both Copland and Bowles did manage to get a fair amount of work done. On 18 September, Bowles wrote to Stein that "the piano has not been such a complete calamity. I have managed to finish my sonata [for oboe and clarinet] and after a few more weeks of copying its parts and the instrumental score for Miss Boulanger to read I can begin to pray nights to have it played."[15] Prayer would hardly have been necessary, as Copland had already decided to include the *Sonata for Oboe and Clarinet* on a 16 December concert in London that he was arranging with Roger Sessions.

(15)
Paul Bowles to Gertrude Stein, 18 September 1931, *IT*, p. 87.

By the end of November Bowles had arrived in Paris to face Copland, Boulanger, and the music—specifically, the premiere of his *Sonata for Oboe and Clarinet*, which was just around
the corner. Shortly after his return to Paris, Bowles received a p. 41
letter from Copland asking for the instrumental parts of the sonata. All that was left to do was the mechanical (but time-consuming) task of copying out the two parts from the score and proof-reading them. Still, the performance in London was less than three weeks away, so Bowles had no time to lose. He wrote to Copland: "I shall start making the parts, but God knows how right they will be. I wish there were some way of your seeing them before I send them to London. Oh dear, oh dear! I insist on getting them done in time for the rehearsals. In fact I should blow up and die immediately if it could not come off on account of lack of time."[16] The London concert, after all, would mark the first important performance of one of his compositions, and the company with whom he shared the program—Thomson,

(16)
Quoted in Copland and Perlis, p. 191.

Sessions, Carlos Chávez, Israel Citkowitz and Copland himself — was genuinely intimidating in its professionalism.

It had always been Copland's hope that Bowles would study with Boulanger, his own teacher and a pedagogue he esteemed above all others. Indeed, Boulanger's studio had become a virtual pilgrimage site: beginning with Virgil Thomson and Copland in the 1920s and extending through Philip Glass in the 1960s, Boulanger taught three generations of American composers. But by late November 1931, Virgil Thomson had entered the picture, and he took a position diametrically opposed to Copland's. Although Copland still idolized Boulanger, Thomson, who had studied with Boulanger in 1921-22, had grown increasingly disillusioned with her. Now he urged Bowles to reconsider Copland's advice. Indeed, Thomson felt that the light touch of the French composer Paul Dukas (today best-remembered for *The Sorcerer's Apprentice* [1897]) would be much better suited to Bowles than the strict, dogmatic method of Boulanger.

Although Bowles had already visited Boulanger and shown her his sonata, she was reluctant to take him on as a
p.42 pupil. Her hesitance is not difficult to understand. Aside from his lessons with Copland, Bowles had had precious little training in composition, and certainly no strict introduction to counterpoint, a skill Boulanger valued above all else. But it is doubtful that Bowles' motives were quite as sterling as he made out to Copland.[17] In fact, he disliked the thought of study with Boulanger, and was seeking to avoid it. "I was delighted [at her rejection of private lessons] because I didn't want to study with her anyway, and it gave me a chance to leave," he recalled recently. "That's all I ever wanted to do." He did make a brief apperance at the École Normale for classes, which he remembered as "utter boredom." [18]

(17)
Paul Bowles to Aaron Copland, 28 November 1931, *IT*, p. 91.

(18)
KRS, 13 July 1993.

And so Bowles never did study with Boulanger, nor did he work with Dukas. In effect, he squandered his one opportunity for a serious, prolonged course in composition—a decision that would leave him, for the rest of his life, feeling like an untrained composer.

Now the premiere of Bowles' *Sonata for Oboe and Clarinet* was at hand. The concert took place on 16 December at Aeolian Hall on Wigmore Street, the program consisting of Bowles' sonata, Thomson's *Capital Capitals* (to Stein's texts), Chávez's *Piano Sonatina*, Sessions' *Piano Sonata*, Citkowitz's settings of Joyce poems, and Copland's *Piano Variations*. It must have been an extraordinary moment of arrival for Bowles, since his sonata was surrounded by works of well-respected and more experienced composers. But their reputations were hardly on the line to the degree that his was. The negative response from the press must have upset him.

In truth, the critics panned the entire concert, not just Bowles' piece. That must have lessened Bowles' disappointment, and by January 1932, when he wrote from Italy to Morrissette, he could describe the critical reaction with a sort of pained hilarity: "The concert had a limited success with its limited audience. George Cattaui of the Egyptian Legation knowing reporters introduced me: scandalous articles! Even a reporter! My picture taken in Tangier for the Evening Standard. All about the Bible, pagan strains with an oboe. Others: you gotta have more skill to put that stuff over on us! Aaron's piece: meaningless and painfully discordant! Virgil's made a great stir: Queerest Stein song! Subhead [referring to Bowles]: Runaway Composer who never saw a Bible. That means so much in England."[19]

(19) Paul Bowles to Bruce Morrissette, January 1931, *IT*, p. 95.

Bowles could not have known that Henry Boys, writing in the January-February 1932 issue of *Modern Music*—the American journal that in a few short years would launch Bowles' own career as a music critic—would also latch onto the sonata's lack of "skill." Boys felt that the sonata had a "sure sense of style, but the workmanship is not yet accomplished enough to deal with such a combination and rather

(20)
Henry Boys, *Modern Music* IX (Jan.-Feb. 1932), p. 92.

matches the immature and superficial mode of thought."[20]

Although Bowles' *Sonata for Oboe and Clarinet* seems to spring forth *sui generis*, its uniqueness is something of an illusion, created by the fact that all his preceding compositions are lost. There is no disputing the fact that it remains an unusual and highly idiosyncratic work—and that a critic like Boys who sensed Bowles' personal voice yet lamented his lack of craftmanship was not entirely wrong.

Although Bowles had studied with Copland throughout the period of the sonata's composition, it sounds not a bit like his teacher. To be sure, Copland communicated many of his aesthetic values to Bowles, and these—an expressive restraint, an economy of means, and a lean, neo-classic orientation—are all present in the sonata. Bowles' choice of two woodwinds would undoubtedly have pleased Copland, who favored an astringency of timbre. But the sonata's pungent austerity is more severe than anything Copland had created.

In 1931, Copland had just completed his *Piano Variations* and was working on his *Short Symphony*, two of

p. 44

the most dissonant and uncompromising compositions of his entire career. Bowles, who adored both works, recalled recently that at this time, "I thought Aaron was synonymous with dissonance."[21] Yet the *Piano Variations*, despite their stab at a Schoenbergian organization of pitch, are still conceived harmonically. In Bowles' *Sonata for Oboe and Clarinet*, the conception is contrapuntal, which is only partly a reflection of the fact that it is scored for two melody instruments. Mostly, one senses that Bowles was inherently drawn to the dry linearity of Thomson's music—and to the nose-thumbing impudence of the group of French composers known as *Les six*, who in turn paid homage to Erik Satie and Dada.

(21)
KRS, 13 July 1993.

The entire three-movement sonata lasts less than eight minutes, an example of economy if ever there was one.

Entirely devoid of expressive or interpretive indications, it already demonstrates an emotional reticence that would become a hallmark of Bowles' instrumental music. The first movement opens with a jaunty, angular theme, and immediately one is struck by the pervasively contrapuntal orientation. So stark and linear is this music that harmonic goals are deliberately avoided, and the tonality is further obscured by the dissonance of the part-writing. Although there are no "pagan strains" in the oboe, both instruments delight in ornamental grace-notes, which occasionally suggest the sound of a North African woodwind like the *rhaita*.

A full break announces the plaintive, newly lyrical second theme, marked at a slower tempo than the first. After a lively quasi-developmental section, there is a reversed recapitulation, which begins with the second theme rather than the first. What has transpired in no more than three minutes is a rare example in Bowles' work of a sonata form.

Bowles' discomfort with sonata form is plain at every juncture. Its sections are set off by pauses and tempo changes, and there is nothing organic about the way they unfold or develop. Instead, they are simply juxtaposed. This modular, transitionless conception of musical form would become an increasingly distinctive trait of Bowles' work; it reaches its apex
in the quasi-cinematic jump-cuts of the *Concerto for Two Pianos* (1946-48).

Bowles is more at ease in the sonata's second movement, a loose, three-part (ABA) song form that would soon become one of his favorite instrumental structures. Tender and yearning in its lyricism, it is less dissonant than the movements that surround it. As for the finale, it owes its conception to an extra-musical circumstance—specifically, Bowles' meeting with the Dada artist and poet Kurt Schwitters.

Back in June 1931, Bowles had made a side-trip from Berlin to Hanover in order to visit Schwitters. Bowles was particularly fascinated by Schwitters' meaningless syllabic poems, one of which went:

Lanke trr gll
Pe pe pe pe pe
Ooka. Ooka. Ooka. Ooka.
Lanke trr gll.

Pi pi pi pi pi.

Tzuuka. Tzuuka. Tzuuka. Tzuuka.

"I notated the words, the rhythm, and the vocal inflections and later used it without changes as the frame for the theme of the rondo movement of a sonata for oboe and clarinet," Bowles has explained. (*WS*:115).

The finale of the sonata opens with an impudent theme that is a literal replication of the rhythms of Schwitters' poem, broken up between the two instruments in a jerky, hocket-like manner. But the promised "rondo movement" never materializes. What Bowles offers is simply a parade of ideas that are every bit as dissonant as those of the first movement (there are plenty of perversely strident sevenths), if not as contrapuntal. The opening Schwitters theme never once returns, as a proper rondo form would require.

The formal peculiarities of the sonata may be explained, in part, by the fact that Bowles composed it sequentially. "One day I'd compose from, say, measure 1 to 8, and I'd play it and change the notes until I finally had it straight," he recalled recently. "Then the next day, I would go from 9 to 15. And that was the way I went." Nothing, it seems, was sketched or
p.46 planned in advance. "I never knew where I was going. But I've always written [prose] that way too, so there's really no difference. After a week of this thing, I probably could play up to measure 25, and add to it little by little. It was an agglomerative form"—he laughed at the made-up term —"but I don't think that exists."[22]

Bowles does not dispute the fact that the *Sonata for Oboe and Clarinet* remains an oddity, inhabiting a uniquely dissonant, contrapuntal sound world. "It seems very peculiar to me, almost as if someone else had written it. It's more like the *Aria, Chorale, and Canonic Rondo* [23] than anything else that came after." When Thomson would write to Copland in 1932 that Bowles' "musical procedure is far too contrapuntal now," [24] he might well have been thinking of this sonata.

(22)

All material on the sonata from KRS, 13 July 1993.

(23)

A lost work dating from 1930.

(24)

Virgil Thomson to Aaron Copland, 17 October 1932, in *Selected Letters of Virgil Thomson*, ed. Tim Page and Vanessa Weeks Page (New York, 1988) , p. 104.

Bowles' description of his compositional method implies not so much a haphazard approach to form as a cultivatedly subconscious one. This obliteration of conscious process (together with the sketching and planning it demands) would become a hallmark of his fiction, even of a novel as vast and labyrinthine as *The Spider's House* (1955). As the years passed, however, Bowles would discover that in music such a surrealist approach would work far better in free-associative, self-generated structures than in the rigorous forms inherited from the Classical masters.

Copland and Bowles were never again as close as they had been during 1931. Copland, agitating by letter from America, continued to believe that Bowles should follow some formal course of instruction, but Thomson now openly sided with Bowles. Thomson wrote to Copland on 17 October 1932 that Bowles "shocks everybody" because he "prefers the life of a *poule de luxe* and he lives quite well that way and gets his work done all the same. You are shocked because he won't follow the conventional education of a young man of talent. He is frightfully impressed by what you tell him and gets awfully worried because he can't do it. But the force of his own genius is stronger than any reason or affection. So with the best will in the world to do as you say and learn the contrapuntal routines, he just can't be bothered." Thomson closed by stating: "I assure you there is nothing to worry about."[25]

(25)
Virgil Thomson to Aaron Copland, 17 October 1932, in Page and Page, pp. 103-4.

Copland must have realized that he was losing this battle, for his exhortations to Bowles to study composition gradually ceased. But he continued to champion Bowles' music, even from afar. When Copland organized the First Festival of Contemporary Music at Yaddo on 30 April and 1 May 1932, he wrote to Bowles in Paris, asking him to contribute something for the concert. Bowles sent six songs to his own texts, [26] his first concentrated effort in the

(26)
The six songs are: *It Was a Long Trip Back, Here I Am, Will You Allow Me to Lie on the Grass, In the Platinum Forest, Things Shall Go On* and *Today, More than Ever*. In

Copland and Perlis, p. 201, Copland mentions that five songs by Bowles were performed at Yaddo, so one of these six may have been omitted from the concert. The fact that a sketch of five of Bowles' songs survives in Copland's hand suggests that only five were performed.

field of song-writing, which in future years would inspire some of his finest works. After the songs were sung at Yaddo by Ada MacLeish (with Copland accompanying), Copland wrote to Bowles exuberantly: "You're on the map now, and don't you forget it." (*WS*:153)

By the summer of 1933, Copland had cajoled Bowles into returning to America. Bowles despised being home, and in June 1933 wrote to Thomson: "Certainly nobody hates N.Y. as much as I do....Why the Hell Aaron advised me to return is more than I know."[27] Apparently Copland warned Bowles to resist the charms of both Morocco and Thomson. Bowles spilled the beans when he quoted Copland's words in a letter to Thomson: "He [Copland] replied that my impatience p.48 was charming and had got me far, 'But don't let it send you rushing back to the arms of Virgil or Abs-dabs-salaam!'"[28]

(27)
Quoted in Caponi, p. 67.

(28)
Paul Bowles to Virgil Thomson, summer 1933, *IT*, p. 121.

Bowles, however, had already begun to gravitate toward Thomson and away from Copland. Copland became increasingly involved with creating an aggressively American music, while Bowles found his aesthetic predilections more in line with those of a cosmopolitan Francophile like Thomson. It was Thomson who helped Bowles secure his first important theatrical commission, the score for the John Houseman/Orson Welles production of *Horse Eats Hat* (1936). It was Thomson who hired Bowles as a music critic for the New York *Herald Tribune*, and who was his boss from November 1942 to February 1946, during which time Bowles penned more than 400 concert reviews and essays for the paper. Indeed, the composer Peggy Glanville-Hicks, who was close to Bowles during the 1940s, virtually dismissed Bowles' relationship with Copland: "If Copland taught him anything it never showed in his music. But his debt to Thomson is considerable....Above all he learned from Thomson not a technical so much as an ideological method of procedure—the dada idea of Erik Satie.... This procedure, a method whereby styles, period mannerisms, all kinds of musical elements alien to one's own style, can be contained within that style, was a usable device, instantly absorbed by Bowles."[29]

(29)
Peggy Glanville-Hicks, "Paul Bowles—The Season of Promise," *Musical America*, 1 November 1949, p. 7 (Reprinted here, pp. 103-117).

Undoubtedly Glanville-Hicks' argument contains a kernel of truth. Still, Bowles and Copland remained fond of one another, and to this day Bowles praises Copland's music, while he denigrates Thomson's. "I worried about disappointing Aaron," Bowles recalled recently. "I didn't worry about not living up to Virgil's expectations, because I didn't think he had any."[30] Although Bowles admired Thomson's settings of Stein, especially the opera *Four Saints in Three Acts* (1934), he states today that, "I never was very attached to Virgil's instrumental music. Perhaps I didn't like his music very much. Certainly I never felt anything for it the way I did for Aaron's music, and I never will."[31]

(30)
KRS, 13 July 1993.

(31)
KRS, 13 July 1993.

Copland, it would seem, returned the affection. In an essay published in *Modern Music* in 1936, Copland defended Bowles against his detractors. "There are those who refuse to see in Bowles anything more than a dilettante," he wrote. Bowles, he felt, had written "music that comes from a fresh personality, music full of charm and melodic invention, at times surprisingly well-made in an instinctive and non-academic fashion. Personally I prefer an 'amateur' like Bowles to your 'well-trained' conservatory product."[32] By now Copland had clearly realized that Bowles would never settle down to some formal training in composition. But Copland had learned to treasure the music that Bowles succeeded in composing, and he never stopped doing so.

(32)
See above, note 1.

A Nomad in New York, 1933-1947

By Gena Dagel Caponi

[The following biographical essay is an abridged version of the central study of Paul Bowles' musical career; for further and more complete information, reference is made to its original form, *Book III of Paul Bowles. Romantic Savage* (Carbondale, 1994).]

Between 1933 and 1947 Paul Bowles was based in New York, where he successfully supported himself composing music for the theater. Bowles returned to New York from North Africa via San Juan, Puerto Rico, in 1933, dragging his feet all the way. From San Juan he wrote Gertrude Stein, "I had no desire to come to America and have no idea why I did now that I am here."[1] From New York, he wrote Virgil Thomson, "certainly nobody hates N.Y. as much as I do....Why the Hell Aaron [Copland] advised me to return is more than I know."[2] Later, from Northampton, Massachusetts, he wrote to Stein, "I am staying in desolate country with an aunt for the summer, working; I must always tell you that, because you never believe it. This was the wrong year to come home. Copland has a new pet [violinist Victor Kraft]....And since he was the only reason for returning, I feel deceived."[3]

(1) Paul Bowles to Gertrude Stein, no date [1933], Beinecke Rare Book Library, Yale University.

(2) Paul Bowles to Virgil Thomson, June 1933, Jackson Music Library, Yale University.

(3) Paul Bowles to Gertrude Stein, no date [1933], Beinecke.

By summer's end, Bowles had repaired his relationship with Copland and made plans to stay a few days with the composer at Lake

George before returning to New York to live with Harry Dunham for the winter. Although Bowles did move into Dunham's East Thirty-eighth Street apartment, he soon moved out, to an apartment on West Fifty-eighth Street. Copland agreed to pay half the rent for the apartment, in exchange for his use of it as a studio and for meetings of his Young Composers Group.

Copland convened the Young Composers Group in 1932 to encourage American music through informal meetings among artists living in New York. The Group soon established an age limit (twenty-five) and on 15 January 1933 presented its first concert at the New School for Social Research. Regular members included Henry Brant, Israel Citkowitz, Lehman Engel, Vivian Fine, Bernard Herrmann, Jerome Moross and Elie Siegmeister. Irregulars included George Antheil, Marc Blitzstein, Carlos Chávez, John Kirkpatrick and Irwin Heilner.[4] During the weekly meetings, Herrmann, Citkowitz and Brant engaged in vociferous and even combative discussions that Bowles found depressing and futile.[5] Exacerbating matters for Bowles was a denigration of the works produced by cosmopolitans. Bowles did not remain with the group when they went to Roger Sessions' harmony classes—he found Sessions, like Nadia Boulanger in Paris, "formidable," and attended only a couple of classes.[6] A short piano piece he composed at the time bears traces of Thomson's technique of creating musical impressions of his colleagues. Bowles' *Portrait of Five* has subtitles that offer verbal impressions of his colleagues: "Virgil Thomson (smiling)"; "Aaron Copland (remembering the world)"; "Roger Sessions (looking careful & honest)"; "George Antheil (in a hurry to go)"; and "Israel Citkowitz (practicing being pleasant)."[7] The music

(4)
Aaron Copland and Vivian Perlis, *Copland: 1900 Through 1942* (New York, 1984), p. 192.

p. 52

(5)
Oscar Levant, *A Smattering of Ignorance* (New York, n.d.), p. 225.

(6)
Paul Bowles, conversation with author, February 1986.

itself consists of "semi-parodies of the styles of the various composers." [8]

(7)
Paul Bowles, *Portrait of Five*, Collection of the Harry Ransom Humanities Research Center, University of Texas at Austin.

(8)
Paul Bowles to author, 25 February 1988.

Upon arriving in New York, Bowles had taken a few pieces to John Kirkpatrick, a friend of Copland and a pianist who specialized in playing new music. Kirkpatrick played Bowles' *Piano Sonatina* for Claire Reis, director of the League of Composers' concerts, and Reis scheduled the work for a concert late in 1933. Reviewing it in *Modern Music*, composer Marc Blitzstein described the sonatina as "what is called damned clever. Whiter than even the White Russians dispense it."

In 1934, however, Bowles had not begun the type of composing that was to provide the bulk of his income throughout the next decade and a half. Bowles soon found himself in serious financial trouble. He tried to concentrate on his work—composing and attending the vocal and instrumental rehearsals for the Virgil Thomson-Gertrude Stein opera, *Four Saints in Three Acts*—but found memories of North African air and light interfering with increasing frequency. Sooner or later, he knew, the opportunity to return would present itself.

That spring Bowles completed a six-song cycle, *Memnon*, on a text by Jean Cocteau. Following Thomson's example he also composed two songs using words from Stein's *Useful Knowledge* ("Scenes from the Door"). Pleased that his compositions were "as different from Virgil's settings as anything could be," he decided to publish them himself, on his own label, Editions de la Vipère.[9]

(9)
Paul Bowles to Gertrude Stein, no date [1934], Beinecke.

Other works published under the Vipère label, a label he used in 1934 and 1935, included compositions by David Diamond and Erik Satie, with art by Anne Miracle, Kristians Tonny, and the Russian painter and scene designer, Eugene Berman.

In June 1934, Bowles left New York for what would turn out to be a briefer stay, principally in Morocco, than he had planned.

Returning via Colombia, he crossed into the Pacific and travelled on to Los Angeles, where he wrote a series of piano preludes and set to music a letter from Gertrude Stein (*Letter to Freddy*). But the most important outcome of Bowles' two months in California—one in Los Angeles and the second with relatives in San Francisco—was a visit to Henry Cowell. Born in California in 1897, Cowell had made his name as a pianist who had performed in Europe and in New York; his work featured tone clusters that he played with his forearms and passages in which harp-like sounds were achieved by playing the strings of the piano directly. Like Bowles, Cowell had educated himself and then, after having composed extensively, decided to take on some formal training with Charles Seeger, who described him as "a very good example of autodidacts all through his life: he never learned anything from anybody else; he appropriated what he liked and paid no attention to what he didn't like."[10] In their approach to training, if not to music, Bowles and Cowell were kindred souls.

(10)
Charles Seeger, quoted in Rita Mead, "The Amazing Mr. Cowell," *American Music* I/4 (Winter 1983), p. 65.

Cowell inspired Bowles and was interested in Bowles' compositions as well as his travels. Bowles sat in on Cowell's rhythm class at Stanford and demonstrated the *claves* he had brought back from his trip. Cowell responded by devoting the April 1935 issue of his *New Music* to works of Bowles and Carlos Chávez. Bowles' new piece, *Letter to Freddy*, appeared along with three other Bowles compositions: *Café Sin Nombre*, Part IV of *Danger de Mort*, and Part II of *Scènes d'Anabase*.

Bowles called 1935 the "nadir" of his life, yet Cowell's April publication of his works marked the beginning of a slow rise in fortune. Later in the year Thomson requested that Bowles provide music for a concert of contemporary music by the Friends and Enemies of Modern Music, an adjunct group to the Hartford Museum, in Hartford, Connecticut. Bowles accepted and, in spite of a disagreement with Thomson, performed his music at least twice that year in Hartford.

In the spring of 1935 Bowles had moved back to New York City, arriving with more than half the score for a ballet that he and Eugene Berman had determined to produce. He and Berman took long walks together along the waterfront discussing the project. Berman's enthusiasm quickly shifted from the ballet to the views of Manhattan he and Bowles saw from the water's edge, and he was soon immersed in a series of paintings that showed the city in ruins. Recognizing they would never finish the ballet, Bowles used much of the music for a 1936 theater production.

Shortly thereafter Lincoln Kirstein asked Bowles to write a new ballet score to be called *Yankee Clipper*, which would reflect Bowles' interest in travel and be choreographed by dancer Eugene Loring. Bowles composed a score drawn from his travels, using "authentic rhythms characteristic of the foreign parts" to be visited by the "New England sailor" in the ballet.[11] Percussion instruments included two African drums, tuned a minor third apart, a bass drum, a *tambour de provence*, a xylophone, timbals, *guiros* and *claves*.[12]

(11)
Program for *Yankee Clipper*, Ballet Caravan, Lincoln Kirstein, Director, HRHRC.

(12)
Paul Bowles, *Yankee Clipper*, HRHRC.

Indigenous music of all countries intrigued the young composer, particularly rhythmically complicated music. Bowles was obsessed with rhythm, in a nearly clinical sense. According to more than one acquaintance, he was always drumming patterns on the table-top or arm of a chair. He had been interested in African-American music since high school, when he began a correspondence with ethnographer John Hammond, and had collected "race" records while a student in Virginia. With Hammond, Bowles went to Harlem to meet young pianist Teddy Wilson; and Bowles returned to Harlem often to listen to music. Bowles was one of the first Americans to review the music of African-American jazz artists in serious publications on a regular basis, and his reviews show an astute ear and a shrewd understanding of the uniqueness of African-Americans' music.

Early in his career, Bowles found occasional support from the New Deal's Works Progress Administration, which had formed several subagencies to provide employment for artists. On 2 April 1936, the Federal Music Project presented an all-Bowles concert, which included his *Sonata for Flute and Piano*; *Trio for Violin, Violin-cello and Piano*; *Suite for Violin and Piano*; *Scènes d'Anabase* and several piano pieces, as well as a presentation of Harry Dunham's film *Venus and Adonis*, with music by Bowles. Reviewer (and composer) Colin McPhee agreed with other members of the audience that the film was "incredibly stupid" but added that "the music carried it along in its allure and melodic individuality."[13]

(13)
Colin McPhee, "New York's Spring Season, 1936," *Modern Music* XIII/ 4 (May-June 1936), p. 40.

The same issue of *Modern Music* that carried McPhee's review held an essay by Aaron Copland on the promising young composers of the day. Answering anticipated criticism, and perhaps countering his own hesitations, Copland wrote, "There are those who refuse to see in Bowles anything more than a dilettante. Bowles himself persists in
p.56 adopting a militantly non-professional air in relation to all music, including his own. If you take this attitude at its face value, you will lose sight of the considerable merit of a large amount of music Bowles has already written. It is music that comes from a fresh personality, music full of charm and melodic invention, at times surprisingly well made in an instinctive and non-academic fashion. Personally I much prefer an 'amateur' like Bowles to your 'well-trained' conservatory product."[14] Bowles had now published in Cowell's *New Music*, had an entire Federal Music Project devoted to his work, and, despite being first an "amateur" dandy and then a rebel rogue, had won the support of McPhee and, more importantly, Copland in *Modern Music*.

(14)
Aaron Copland, "America's Young Men —Ten Years Later," *Modern Music* XIII/ 4 (May-June 1936), p. 10.

In July 1936, Bowles joined in the outpouring of sympathy for the republican government fighting Franco in Spain by helping to form the Committee of Republican Spain, which raised two thousand dollars for the Madrid government through their production *Who Fights This Battle?* Bowles wrote the score for Kenneth White's script, which was directed by Joseph Losey, with Earl Robinson serving as music director.

Even though he was increasingly active as a composer, Bowles still had little in the way of regular income. Things on this front changed when Virgil Thomson stepped in and gave him a useful introduction to Orson Welles. Along with John Houseman, Welles had gone to work for Project 891 or the Classical Theatre, one of half a dozen theatrical units of the Federal Theater Project. Welles and Houseman had turned their attention to a French play, *The Italian Straw Hat*, which had been made into a silent film by one of Welles' favorite directors, René Clair. Edwin Denby translated the 1851 Eugène Labiche work, and Welles and Houseman transformed it into a surrealist farce. Bowles' music helped establish a frantic pace similar to that of Keystone Kops silent films.

Bowles had no experience in orchestral music, so Thomson helped him assemble and then orchestrate an elaborate score—"overtures, intermezzos, meditations, marches, even a song or two"—from works Bowles had already written, including the abandoned Berman ballet.[15] The play, called *Horse Eats Hat*, opened at the Maxine Elliot Theater in October; one critic declared the production a "demented piece of surrealism perilously close to being a genuine work of art."[16]

(15)
Virgil Thomson, *Virgil Thomson* (New York, 1966), p. 265.

(16)
Quoted in John Houseman, *Entertainers and the Entertained. Essays on Theater, Film, and Television* (New York, 1986), p. 19.

Horse Eats Hat led to a Project 891-Welles production, also staged at the Maxine Elliot Theater: Christopher Marlowe's *Tragical History of Dr. Faustus*. This vehicle for Welles' genius and his fascination with magic demanded a total of seventy-six lighting cues and sound effects, including a scene in which a pig, a side of beef, two chickens, and a pudding fly off the dinner table and pirouette and then disappear into black velvet drapes.[17] Bowles alone wrote the music for the production, Thomson being in France, and the play enjoyed huge success. The New York *Times* estimated that in the first five months following its 18 January 1937 opening, more than eighty thousand people saw the standing-room-only show. In the theater, Bowles found both a new and an unexpected source of income and an outlet for expression in which he was particularly talented.

(17)
Charles Higham, *Orson Welles. The Rise and Fall of an American Genius* (New York, 1985), p. 90.

In the winter of 1937, Bowles announced his intention of resigning from the Federal Theater Project and travelling to Mexico. Berman accused him of being irresponsible, a criticism that had never previously dissuaded Bowles. After printing fifteen thousand anti-Trotsky stickers to take along, Bowles set out. In Mexico City, Bowles used a note of introduction from Copland to meet the composer Silvestre Revueltas and heard for the first time Revueltas' *Homenaje a García Lorca*. He spent some time with Revueltas and through him met p.58 the Mexican composers called the Grupo de los Cuatro: Daniel Ayala, Pablo Moncayo, Salvador Contreras, and Blas Galindo. Revueltas served as Bowles' guide to the world of Mexican music and composers.

Soon thereafter, Bowles left for a tour of the wilderness of Tehuantepec in southern Mexico, which he found even more beautiful and hostile than the Sahara, and celebrated May Day with Zapotecans who asked him to teach them about communism. Back in Mexico City, Bowles received a wire from Lincoln Kirstein saying that the ballet *Yankee Clipper* was to be presented in Philadelphia and that Bowles was needed to orchestrate the score.

Trouble with orchestration plagued Bowles. He managed to pull together an orchestral version of *Yankee Clipper* by having Harry Brant concentrate on the ship scenes while Bowles did the ports-of-call. Rena Bowles, John Latouche, Marian Chase, and Jane Auer accompanied him on the trip to Philadelphia, where Alexander Smallens conducted the piece on a program that included *Filling Station* by Virgil Thomson, and *Pocahontas* by Elliott Carter, who called the "tuneful" sailor dances Bowles' "best music...pastiches of the exotica."[18] The critic Paul Rosenfeld asserted, "it is music of a kind that no civilized community can do without. It is hard of edge and light in content, music in kid gloves, the music of a dandy."[19]

(18)
Elliott Carter, "With the Dancers," *Modern Music* XV/2 (January-February 1938), p. 122.

(19)
Paul Rosenfeld, "The Newest American Composers," *Modern Music* XV/3 (March-April 1938), p. 158.

For the next several months, Bowles was as peripatetic in New York as he had been in North Africa and Mexico. During the summer he spent some time with Kristians Tonny, Tonny's wife Marie-Claire Ivanoff, and Chase at his Uncle Charles' lake house at Glenora. He was working on a new piece: *Denmark Vesey*, an opera with a libretto by Charles-Henri Ford for an all-black cast, concerning the 1822 Charleston slave conspiracy led by a former slave named Denmark Vesey. Returning to New York in October, Bowles took up residence in the Chelsea Hotel and worked on the opera in Edwin Denby's loft on Twenty-first Street. He devoted prodigious effort to *Vesey*, which in letters to Ford he often called his "baby." By January, the first act was presented by the Juanita Hall Choir at a benefit for *New Masses*.[20]

Even unfinished, the opera was impressive enough for Virgil Thomson to call it one of the three best "unperformed" American operas, a status above which, sadly, it never rose.[21] In 1939, the Juanita Hall singers again presented the first act, along with part of Act II, giving Bowles "a chance to show my teeth above a white tie and hang my head before applause," but meanwhile, he reported to Ford that Du Bose Heyward had stolen the idea of Denmark Vesey for an opera of his own, called "Don't You Want To Be Free?"[22] As a result, Bowles resolved not to give the script to any

(20)
Juanita Hall was later to become famous as Bloody Mary in *South Pacific*. For now she led her nine singers in a chorus.

(21)
Virgil Thomson, *Selected Letters of Virgil Thomson*, ed. Tim Page and Vanessa Weeks Page, (New York, 1988), p. 154.

(22)
Paul Bowles to Charles-Henri Ford, 10 January 1939; no date [spring 1939], HRHRC.

(23)
Paul Bowles to Charles-Henri Ford, no date [spring 1939]; 13 December 1947; 22 March [1948], HRHRC.

(24)
Paul Bowles to Charles-Henri Ford, 25 January [1948], HRHRC.

more “Broadway people”; then, inexplicably in 1945, he gave his only copy of the score to tenor Romolo de Spirito for a recording by Disc.[23] Two years later Ford hoped to finish it and wrote to Bowles asking whether he could write a final act. He sent Bowles the script, but Bowles responded, “Of course it’s a wonderful scenario, but what good does it do me, when my score appears to have been completely lost by De Spirito?”[24]

Because he moved so often, taking only clothing and books with him, Bowles frequently lost track of items stored, packed, or otherwise uprooted. Meticulous as he was about his own appearance, he seems to have taken a cavalier attitude toward his belongings. Many of Bowles’ theater scores were lost because companies kept the scores themselves rather than return them to the composer. “It wasn’t only the Federal Works

p. 60

Projects that kept scores after productions had closed; Broadway did it, too. And of course at that time one had to have music Photostatted in order to keep a copy, and it cost 75 cents a page for negative and positive, and that was too much, or so I thought. In any case, now I have nothing.”[25]

(25)
Paul Bowles to Virgil Thomson, 6 December 1976, Jackson.

Bowles’ film scores, as well, disappeared. French surrealists were among the most artistic in creating a union of film and music, and Bowles followed their work with enthusiasm. Erik Satie’s music for the Francis Picabia and René Clair film *Entre’acte* and Georges Auric’s music to Cocteau’s *La Vie d’un Poète* provided contemporary composers with examples for the relatively new medium. In the late 1930s, several American composers began experimenting with writing for the new media—film and radio—in order to secure a broader audience for American music. The documentary film was a new genre that lent itself particularly well to serious music.

As a composer, Bowles monitored the state of film music in the United States and abroad.[26] He began his own work for film in 1933 with the score for Harry Dunham's short and what Bowles called "lurid" film, *Bride of Samoa. Venus and Adonis* (1935) was their second film. Bowles worked with Swiss-born experimental filmmaker Rudy Burckhardt on two films in 1936: *Seeing the World* and *145 West 21*, the second of which referred to Edwin Denby's address and captured the acting talents of John Latouche and of Aaron Copland as a roofer. Two years later Bowles scored two more Burckhardt films: *Chelsea Through the Magnifying Glass* and *How to Become a Citizen of the U.S.*, which Burckhardt remembers being screened "somewhere in Brooklyn in a room that couldn't be made dark in the daytime" and hearing "one Brooklyn woman saying: 'I can't see a thing but I'm sure it's subversive.'"[27]

(26)
See Bowles' articles on film music in the *Herald Tribune* for 17 January, sec. 6, p. 7; 31 January, sec. 7, p. 7; 29 June, sec. 6, p. 6; and 21 November, sec. 4, p. 6, all from 1943; and in *Modern Music*, from 1939 through 1941, when he wrote "On the Film Front" for each quarterly issue.

(27)
Rudy Burckhardt to author, 15 June 1988.

Sadly, most of Bowles' music was recorded on acetate records instead of being added to the films as a soundtrack. By the 1960s these had disintegrated, and Bowles had kept neither written nor mental notes of the specific scores.[28] This kind of casualness with regard to his own work contrasts dramatically with the otherwise near-compulsive habits of someone who, by his own admission, "lived by immutable self-imposed rules." (*WS*:191)*

(28)
Rudy Burckhardt to author, 15 June 1988.

In 1936, Bowles lived at several addresses in New York; throughout, he maintained a studio on the East River at 2 Water Street in Brooklyn, which had two rooms and a piano and served as "general headquarters." The neighborhood surrounding Water Street was known as Brooklyn Heights and had been home to a score of notables, from Thomas Paine, Henry Ward Beecher, and Alfred Kazin to Hart Crane, Thomas Wolfe, John Dos Passos, and Marianne Moore. Oliver Smith settled in

* REFERENCES TO Paul Bowles, *Without Stopping* (NEW YORK, 1972) ARE CITED WITHIN THE BODY OF THE TEXT AS (*WS*).

Brooklyn Heights for life. Bowles' Water Street studio, however, belonged more to the waterfront itself than to the literary neighborhood. From it one could taste the salt in the air, feel the winds of the sea, and remember that Manhattan was still an island. Close to "silent miles of warehouses with shuttered wooden windows, docks resting on the water like sea spiders,"[29] the studio brought Bowles to a watery wasteland, a New York equivalent of the desolation of North Africa.

(29)
Truman Capote, "Brooklyn Heights: A Personal Memoir," *Holiday* (February 1959), quoted in Susan Edmiston and Linda D. Cirino, *Literary New York: A History and Guide* (Boston, 1976), p. 114.

Bowles' growing friendship at this time with Jane Auer may have limited the time he spent composing. In the summer of 1937 they "began to spin fantasies about how amusing it would be to get married and horrify everyone, above all, [their] respective families." (*WS*:207) On 22 February 1938, they did so in a Dutch Reformed church in New York and left shortly afterwards on a honeymoon trip to Central America and Europe. After several weeks travelling through Panama, Costa Rica, and Guatemala, the Bowleses sailed for Paris.

Not long after the couple had settled in Èze some months later, Bowles received a wire saying Welles needed him
p. 62 in New York to score a production of *Too Much Johnson* at the Mercury Theatre. Paul and Jane moved their considerable collection of luggage back to New York and he began work on the score, for which, as he informed Ford, "there is a hell of a lot of music."[30] Then Welles changed his mind and decided instead to present another play, *Danton's Death*. The decision left Bowles with a one-hundred-dollar honorarium and his music. The latter he converted to a chamber piece titled "Music for a Farce." Nearly half a century later Bowles bitterly remembered the uprooting from Èze as "the most expensive trip I ever took."[31]

(30)
Paul Bowles to Charles-Henri Ford, no date [1938], HRHRC.

(31)
Paul Bowles, conversation with author, February 1986.

Paul and Jane settled in the Chelsea Hotel, and he took up work in Friedrich Kiesler's studio at 57 Seventh Avenue (Kiesler was an Austrian architect and stage designer). They had spent all their money on their lease in France, the theater commission had evaporated, and the cost of living was much higher in New York than in Èze. Bowles needed a steady income and with the help of a sympathetic investigator, he was able to get on the WPA rolls as a composer, for which he wrote pieces on demand and was paid $23.86 a week. Eventually, since Bowles still had his Water Street studio, they were able to get food once a week from the Brooklyn relief board.

In the spring of 1939, Bowles' fortune changed for the better. He received an offer from Robert Lewis of The Group Theatre to write the score for William Saroyan's *My Heart's in the Highlands*. One piece that survives from this score is a song with lyrics by Saroyan, *A Little Closer, Please," (The Pitchman's Song)*. From a pleading, lyrical beginning, the piece launches into a raucous, burlesque hall chorus of "Come a little closer, please," with stride piano punctuating the words perfectly and humorously.

In the autumn Bowles moved to a room in Columbia Heights in Brooklyn, while Jane stayed a while longer at the farmhouse they had rented near Prince's Bay, Staten Island. About this time, Bowles was asked to collaborate on *Love's Old Sweet Song*, another Saroyan play. It was also produced by the p.63 powerful Theatre Guild, a firm of Broadway producers that commanded theater leases and subscription audiences on Broadway from the 1920s through the 1940s.

His next employer was a New Deal agency, the Soil Erosion Service, which was making a film on problems related to soil erosion in the Rio Grande Valley. In New Mexico Bowles researched the area and made notes for scoring *Roots in the Soil*, while working with the filmmaker, Richard Boke. By the spring he had finished the score, and then he and Jane left for Mexico, where he planned to remain for some time.

The Theatre Guild, however, interrupted his respite in late summer, asking him to return to New York to compose the incidental music for a production of Shakespeare's *Twelfth Night*, in which Helen Hayes played Viola and Maurice Evans played Malvolio. Bowles chose an idiom "meant to sound like antique and intricate chamber music," and the score was his greatest success to date. (*WS*:230) *Twelfth Night* had just opened when Theresa Helburn of the Theatre Guild gave Bowles the manuscript to Philip Barry's *Liberty Jones*, an "extravaganza" with one hundred and fifty-eight musical cues in the score. To support this, Bowles' instrumentation included two clarinets (alternate bass clarinet), two trumpets (alternate trombone), one electric violin, one electric guitar, one bass, one harp, two pianos (alternate Hammond organ and celesta), and drums.

Bowles had planned to return to Mexico within six weeks, but the Theatre Guild asked him to write the music to yet another play, Lillian Hellman's *Watch on the Rhine*. Bowles worked on *Watch on the Rhine* through the winter of 1940-41, and then, engaged for a ballet by Lincoln Kirstein, moved with Jane to 7 Middagh Street, "a strange house in Brooklyn Heights, a kind of artists' commune."[32] This "ram-shackle, remodelled four-story brownstone," which was said to resemble a Swiss chalet, became home to a number of literary figures indulging in a successful experiment in communal living. Bowles and his wife, newly returned from Mexico, moved into rooms vacated by Gypsy Rose Lee. They shared the second floor with Oliver Smith and the house itself with W. H. Auden, Benjamin Britten, and Peter Pears, who lived on the third floor, and Thomas Mann's younger son Golo, who lived in the attic. Anaïs Nin called the house "amazing ... like some of the houses in Belgium, the north of France or Austria ... filled with old American furniture.... a museum of Americana."[33] Amid second-hand furniture that he labelled "nineteenth-century American Ugly," Bowles worked on his ballet *Pastorela* for Kirstein's American Ballet Caravan, writing music inspired by the Christmas *posadas* he had heard sung by Mexicans. Bowles placed vocal sequences, using "actual words and melodies" of the *posadas*, throughout the score, composing on an upright piano he installed behind a furnace in the "freezing and airless" cellar. Benjamin Britten monopolized the

p. 64

(32)
Paul Bowles, "Autobiography," *Antaeus* LV (Autumn 1985), p. 16.

(33)
Anaïs Nin, *Diary 1939-1944*, in Edmiston and Cirino, pp. 348-53.

Steinway he had installed in the first-floor salon.[34]

(34)
Edmiston and Cirino, p. 353. The first suite for this work is in the HRHRC dated "1941 New York-Taxco."

In the spring of 1940, Bowles applied to the Guggenheim Foundation for a fellowship in music. It was his third application. He had been encouraged this time to specify the category of "creative music," and proposed an opera with a libretto by William Saroyan. Saroyan, who claimed never to have been to the opera, had written and mailed Bowles his script, entitled *Opera! Opera!* while Bowles was in Albuquerque working on *Roots in the Soil*. Although Bowles looked through the libretto, he made little progress with it over the next year, turning instead to commissioned work: *Twelfth Night*, *Liberty Jones* and *Watch on the Rhine*.

Bowles received one of six Guggenheims in music awarded in March 1941.[35] The money from this award, added to weekly royalties and a few other commissions, meant he could afford to concentrate solely on the opera. He and Jane returned to Taxco in Mexico. Shortly before he left, Katharine Hepburn had asked Bowles whether he would be interested in writing music for a play her brother, Richard, was writing. The script, *Love Like Wildfire*, was waiting for him in Taxco. The rest of the spring he worked on songs for Hepburn's lyrics.

(35)
Other recipients were Marc Blitzstein, David Diamond, Alvin Etler, Hunter Johnson, and Earl Robinson.

By the autumn, Bowles had begun work on the opera, first with Saroyan's libretto.[36] By December he had switched to sections from García Lorca's *Así que Pasen Cinco Años*, in an effort to construct a *zarzuela*, a Spanish form of musical theater consisting of loosely connected songs and dances. Throughout the winter and spring Bowles worked on the *zarzuela*, which he had decided to call *The Wind Remains*.

(36)
Jane Bowles to Virgil Thomson, October 1941, Jackson.

Bowles returned to the United States in the summer of 1942, and on 30 March 1943 The Museum of Modern Art presented the opera, one of a series of "Serenades" of rare music, ancient and modern, which Yvonne de Casa Fuerte had organized. Bowles asked young Leonard Bernstein to conduct the work.[37] The producer and director of the opera was Schuyler Watts. Oliver Smith designed the set, Kermit Love the costumes and Merce Cunningham provided choreography and danced a solo part. Bowles described his creation in a notebook, as follows:

(37)
On the same program, Bernstein conducted *Homenaje a García Lorca* by Silvestre Revueltas, which Bowles had first heard in Mexico five years earlier.

> "The text of *The Wind Remains* is a contraction of García Lorca's most personal and incidentally controversial play . . . its Surrealist technique fitted it for the fragmentary kind of treatment I wanted to give it. I wanted to make of it an intensified and prototypical *zarzuela*, where the thread of dramatic action motivated by dream logic on which the songs and dances are strung becomes scarcely discernible. I translated into English what was not to be sung, leaving the songs in the original Spanish. In the writing of the score I was intent on transferring into musical terms the essence of García Lorca's
> p. 66 poetic language—its textural delicacy, the freshness of its imagery and sound, the subtlety with which it attains an effect of naturalness. It was not part of my desire to write music that sounded Spanish; it seemed to me that if the music were like the text it would end up by being Spanish in the way I wanted it to be. The electric violin [used previously in *Twelfth Night* and *Liberty Jones*] and the wind-machine are the two important sound-makers, dramatically speaking, as the final lines of the play suggest: *Queda el viento/Y la música de tu violín.* (The wind remains/And the music from your violin)."[38]

Thomson was more pleased with the work than Bowles. It was "partly in

(38)
Paul Bowles, Works 7, HRHRC. The work has been published by American Music Edition. Bowles prepared a condensed version of *The Wind Remains* for Peggy Glanville-Hicks' annual New Works for Chamber Orchestra concert at the New York Metropolitan Museum of Art. The concert took place on 19 February 1957, and about a week later the piece was recorded by MGM, with Carlos Surinac conducting the MGM Chamber Orchestra (E3549).

prose and partly in verse, partly spoken and partly sung, partly in English and partly (the verse parts) left in Spanish. It was also partly acted and partly danced. The whole thing was quite beautiful but in an artistic sense only partly successful; largely, I think, because the free form of the *zarzuela* is unacceptable to English-speaking audiences."[39]

(39)
Thomson, p. 339.

"The trouble with the opera," Bowles writes in his autobiography, "was that its text was an excerpt from a Surrealist play. It meant nothing and went nowhere; nor was it an opera, but rather a zarzuela with solo songs, spoken dialogue, instrumental sections, dances and choruses."(*WS*:249) He had received a Guggenheim, written his opera, and seen it premiered in New York. Reviews were good. But Bowles felt dissatisfied and began to wonder whether he wanted to continue this way in music and in New York.

Thomson had dubbed Bowles' immediate circle the "'Little Friends,' all young and a quarter mad." Bowles and Dunham constituted the "founding fathers," along with Latouche; Marian Chase, who married Harry Dunham; Marian's p.67
friend, the wealthy Theodora Griffis, who later married John Latouche; Jane Bowles; and Kristians Tonny. A strange fatality pursued the Little Friends: Dunham was shot down in Borneo in 1943; Griffis died young of cancer; Latouche died of a heart attack at the age of forty; Marian died of polio; and Jane Bowles suffered a debilitating stroke in her early forties. According to Thomson, the group broke up in 1938 with the Tonnys' departure for Europe, Dunham's leaving to photograph the Spanish Civil War, and Jane and Paul's departure for Panama.[40] The disintegration of this group seemed to mark the end of an era for Thomson, and he too decided to leave New York.

(40)
Thomson, p. 280.

After their unrewarded return from France in 1938, the Bowleses continued to spend time with the Little Friends, but their circle gradually widened to cut across the disciplines of theater, dance, music, and literature, touching many influential and significant figures of the period. Thomson, Latouche, the theatrical designer Oliver Smith, dance critic and poet Edwin Denby, playwrights Tennessee Williams and William Saroyan, and young conductor and composer Leonard Bernstein were Bowles' professional associates and his close and valued friends. They met regularly with other artists at the home of Kirk and Constance Askew. In 1943 they spent several weekends with composers Samuel Barber and Gian-Carlo Menotti at their home, Capricorn, in Mount Kisco, New York, where a number of artists passed through. In Manhattan, Paul and Jane dined occasionally with Xenia and John Cage, and Bowles remembers Cage as one of the true innocents he has known in his life. Bowles had met Bernstein at a birthday party for Aaron Copland in 1937; Bowles asked Bernstein to conduct the premiere performance of *The Wind Remains*, and Bernstein dedicated to Bowles the fourth of his *Seven Anniversaries*, a suite of piano pieces for seven people whom he loved.[41]

Peggy Glanville-Hicks, an Australian composer who
p. 68 has been described as "90 pounds of very intense opinion," became one of Bowles' closest friends in the mid-forties. From 1945 until Bowles left for Morocco, they were "almost constant" companions. (*WS*:259) Glanville-Hicks was unusual in that not only was she a composer but she served as an organizer for contemporary music in New York in the 1940s and 1950s. She coordinated concerts, arranged financial support, and wrote criticism, including several articles praising Bowles' music. As a passionate and tireless worker for whatever cause she embraced, Glanville-Hicks kept Bowles' name in circulation in New York even after he had left that city. She also supervised the recording of his *Concerto for Two Pianos* while he was in Morocco.

In New York visibility was a key to success. Consequently, in November 1942, Bowles accepted Virgil Thomson's offer to join the staff of the *Herald Tribune* as music critic, where he and

(41)
Joan Peyser, *Bernstein: A Biography* (New York, 1987), p. 118.

Arthur Berger replaced staff gone for military service. Thomson's advice was succinct: "Just tell 'em what happened, baby. That's all they want to know. Nobody cares about your opinion. Who are you?"[42] The job provided Bowles with a small but steady monthly income and gave him perhaps his first confirmation that he could earn money through writing. Whatever the reasoning, taking the job at the *Herald Tribune* accounted more than any other single factor for the music that Bowles did compose during the decade. "It was a constructive step, inasmuch as it obliged me to remain in New York for the next several years and thus to lead a life which was largely musical."[43]

(42)
Paul Bowles, conversation with author, 13 February 1986.

(43)
Paul Bowles, "Autobiography," p. 17.

Between 1943 and 1947, Bowles wrote music for twelve plays, beginning with two in 1943: Dorothy Heyward's premusical *South Pacific* and John Ford's *'Tis Pity She's a Whore*. Over the course of three days in 1944 Bowles wrote and orchestrated the music to Tennessee Williams' new play, *The Glass Menagerie*, one of his most successful theater scores.

It is difficult to judge Bowles' theater music, because it was so ephemeral. One must accept the word of one of America's most astute critics, Thomson, and believe that Bowles' gift for the theater was every bit as rich as his talent in the American song. Thomson claimed that Bowles "had a unique gift for the theater. It's something you either have or you don't, and Bowles did."[44] In 1946 alone, he wrote music for six different plays. One of his last works of the forties was for Tennessee Williams' *Summer and Smoke*, for which he used the Hammond Novachord (a forerunner of the synthesizer), along with violin, harp, cello, bass clarinet, Chinese drum, cymbals, gong, and snare. Bowles actually returned to New York from Morocco to work on the score, having just finished his first novel.

(44)
Virgil Thomson, conversation with author, 1 October 1984.

In addition to his collaborations with Williams for the theater, Bowles wrote several songs to lyrics by the playwright, among them *Blue*

Mountain Ballads (1946), a suite containing some of Bowles' most natural sounding music. He wrote some of his best music for the voice, including his *Scènes d'Anabase*, the songs to Stein, García Lorca, Charles I, Frances Frost, C.-H. Ford, Seamus O'Sullivan, Richard Thoma, and the *zarzuela The Wind Remains*. Although Bowles expressed many reservations about American civilization, his music shows that he was most at home composing in the American idiom.

Like many composers in the 1930s, Bowles had participated in several government-assisted projects. In the 1940s, as the nation moved out of the Depression, the source of funds shifted from public to private support from commissions and foundations. In addition to the income he earned from theater work and the Guggenheim grant, Bowles found several individual patrons for his works. One such patron was the Marqués de Cuevas. At a party at his home, the marqués revealed to Bowles his idea for a collaboration between Bowles and Salvador Dalí. The subject for the envisioned ballet was a poem by Paul Verlaine, "Dans un vieux parc solitaire et glace. . . ." After signing a contract, Bowles worked out the music and its orchestration, then flew to Mexico for a month's vacation. When he returned, orchestra rehearsals for the ballet,
p. 70 *Colloque Sentimentale*, had begun.

Bowles also found financial backing from such divergent sources as Peggy Guggenheim, Libby Holman, and the exiled Belgian government of the Congo. In the spring of 1943, Guggenheim's *Art of This Century* record series recorded Bowles' *Flute Sonata*. The film *Congo* (1944), for which Bowles wrote the score, was a joint effort among Bowles, Latouche, and filmmaker André Cauvin. Bowles salved his conscience for support of colonialism by reminding himself that Paul Robeson had agreed to provide narration.

Another patron was Paul and Jane's good friend, Libby Holman, the original torch singer made famous by the song "Body and Soul" in the 1930 play *Three's a Crowd*. Holman had talked about an opera she wanted Bowles to write for her and later, when she visited Bowles in Morocco, they decided on García Lorca's three-act poem *Yerma*. Bowles did not finish the opera until 1958, by which time he had lost enthusiasm and the moment had passed for the match between Holman and *Yerma*.

Some of Bowles' most successful music came about through the patronage of duo pianists Arthur Gold and Robert Fizdale. After hearing Bowles' *Nocturne* for two pianos in the 1930s, they asked him whether he would be interested in writing a piece for them. Over time they commissioned three major works: *Sonata for Two Pianos* (1946), *Concerto for Two Pianos, Winds and Percussion* (1947-48), and *A Picnic Cantata* (1953).[45]

(45)
The HRHRC holds the score for *A Picnic Cantata;* the *Sonata for Two Pianos* was published by G. Schirmer in 1949. The *Concerto for Two Pianos, Winds and Percussion* is alternately called *Concerto for Two Pianos;* an orchestral version is called *Concerto for Two Pianos and Orchestra*. Both versions have parts on rental from American Music Edition.

The *Sonata for Two Pianos* turned out to be one of the showiest works for piano that Bowles wrote. Its first movement is nonmelodic, jazzy, and percussive, with the Debussy-like repetitive phrasing that is characteristic of Bowles' music. The second movement is impressionistic, at times bluesy, and the entirely rhythmic third movement (with a repeating rhythmic figure borrowed from his ballet *Yankee Clipper*) features the pianos as percussion instruments at a length that is unique in Bowles' scores. Although Bowles wrote that he was "rather ashamed of it" because "the style seemed wrong," this movement is among Bowles' most progressive work, improving upon Cowell's piano-percussion experiments and pre-dating the works of minimalists such as Steve Reich and John Adams by two decades.[46]

(46)
Paul Bowles to author, 5 November 1988.

Bowles began his second Gold and Fizdale commission, the *Concerto for Two Pianos, Winds and Percussion*, during the summer of 1946 in a beach house in Southampton, where he and Jane were guests of John Uihlein, a friend of Jane. Away from New York City, the calm of these surroundings gave Bowles the proper setting in which to compose a long, serious work. He writes, "Only in such serenity could I have found the theme I was looking for with which to open my Concerto. It came one morning after I had drawn a bath and shut the water off. The taps continued to drip, and the theme was in the succession of drops of water as they fell into the tub." (*WS*:266)

Gold and Fizdale premiered the concerto in November 1948, with an ensemble conducted by Lukas Foss. Percussion instruments included marimba, cigar box, and milk bottle, combining to produce an effect one listener compared to a *gamelan*. Critics noted the "complicated African rhythms, and bizarre instrumental combinations of the opening Allegro movement."[47] Arthur Berger preferred the "languorous" quality of the concerto, an effect he thought Bowles actually achieved more successfully in his *Sonata for Two Pianos*, yet decided that "the very choice sonorities, the montage and timing in the sequence of the primitive and jazzy ideas in the other movements he has never surpassed."[48]

People who know Bowles through only his music or only his writing often are surprised to learn of his accomplishments in the other medium and wonder what his work in the
p.72 two areas can possibly have in common. His music is charming, sophisticated, and always entertaining, while his fiction can be horrifying and grim. Yet in both art forms, Bowles exercised the same economy of style. He chose his notes as carefully as he did his words and seldom repeated phrases in order to develop his musical ideas. What interested him most in writing music was much the same as what he sought in his prose: to evoke in the listener or reader a particular emotional state through his art, to entrance his audience and bring them to the subconscious state of being in which his art could have its most powerful effect.

During his years in New York Bowles discovered that incidental music for theater provided the "perfect medium for carrying out some of the ideas [he] had subconsciously been trying to express.... Here, and in writing for films too, one can with immunity write climaxless music, hypnotic music in one of the exact senses of the word, in that it makes

(47)
"Gold and Fizdale Play Five New Works," New York *Times*, 15 November 1948, p. 22.

(48)
Arthur F. Berger, "Duo-Pianists," New York *Herald Tribune*, 15 November 1948.

(49)
American Composers Today. A Biographical and Critical Guide, compiled and ed. by David Ewen (New York, 1949), s.v. "Bowles, Paul."

its effect without the spectator's being aware of it."[49] With incidental music Bowles was free to create a mood without any pressure to develop the music formally beyond its evocative ability. Yet Bowles was unsatisfied with writing incidental music even though, economically, it suited him. He managed to write a substantial amount of chamber music and nonincidental theater music, such as opera and ballets, but he wrote most of it on commission. By 1947 Bowles had lost his taste for writing the one form of music that he knew he could depend on for income. Looking back on the decade, he reflected: "It is true that I 'produced' during those years, but in such a way that I always seemed to find myself doing what someone else wanted done. I furnished music which would embellish or interpret the ideas of others....The malign effects of writing too much gradually became apparent during the spring. I was made aware of a slowly increasing desire to step outside the dance in which inadvertently I had become involved." (*WS*:273-74)

MUSIC

BY VIRGIL THOMSON

BOWLES'

TWELFTH NIGHT

MUSIC

(New York Herald Tribune, 20 November 1940)

p. 74 IT IS MR. BOWLES' GIFT AS A COMPOSER TO WRITE THEATER MUSIC OF PINPOINT DELICACY THAT IS SO PRECISE IN ITS FUNCTIONAL DESIGN AND SO ACCURATE IN ITS ADJUSTMENT TO THE SUBJECT OF EACH PLAY THAT IT HITS HIS AUDIENCE SQUARELY IN BOTH EARS AND RINGS THE BELL FOR THE PLAY AT EVERY MUSIC CUE. WITH SIX MUSICIANS — FLUTE, OBOE, HARP, IMITATION HARPSICHORD, PERCUSSION AND, VERY OCCASIONALLY, A MUTED TRUMPET — HE MAKES A RICH AND ANCIENT-SOUNDING ENSEMBLE THAT IS MORE SUFFICIENT THAN A LARGER GROUP WOULD BE OF MORE DISPARATE SONORITIES.

HE MAKES NO EFFORT TO FILL THE HOUSE WITH NOISE OR TO DOMINATE THE APPLAUSE BETWEEN SCENES. EVEN IF THE MUSIC GETS LOST FOR A MOMENT OR TWO, THAT IS BETTER THAN ANY UNNECESSARY STRIDENCY. HE KEEPS RIGIDLY WITHIN HIS CHOSEN LIMIT, THEREBY GAINING POWER.

THE BOWLES FORMULA WAS ALREADY COMPLETE IN "DR. FAUSTUS" [1936]. HE WRITES NO BRASSY PIT-MUSIC, NO OFF-STAGE REALISTIC SOUND-EFFECTS. HE DOES WHAT NEARLY EVERY MUSICIAN IN THE WORLD WOULD SAY, ON PRINCIPLE, CAN'T BE DONE. HE WRITES CHAMBER-MUSIC TO ACCOMPANY LARGE THEATRICAL PRODUCTIONS, AND HE AGGRAVATES HIS SUPPOSED ERROR BY PUTTING THAT CHAMBER-MUSIC DOWN IN THE PIT. IN "DR. FAUSTUS" HE USED SEVEN MEN UNDER AN APRON.

THE REASON HIS MUSIC DOES NOT DISAPPEAR FROM ALL AUDIBILITY LIES IN HIS CHOICE OF INSTRUMENTS AND HIS MANNER OF SCORING. HE USES ONLY SHARP AND INCISIVE TIMBRES; HE WRITES A TRUE MELODIC PART FOR EACH; AND HE NEVER DOUBLES, NEVER UPSETS HIS SONOROUS EQUILIBRIUM BY MAKING ONE LINE HEAVIER THAN ANOTHER.

ALL HIS EMPHASIS COMES FROM CONTRAST OF TUNE AND TIMBRE, FROM STRUCTURE AND HARMONIC PROGRESS, NEVER FROM WEIGHT. HE LEAVES THAT TO THE ACTORS. IF THEY WANT TO SHOUT AND WHISPER, THAT IS THEIR BUSINESS. MR. BOWLES SETS A PLAY TO MUSIC AS A PRINTER SETS UP AN AUTHOR'S MANUSCRIPT. HE MAKES IT CLEAR AND CLEAN AND COMPREHENSIBLE, FRAMES IT WITH APPROPRIATE INITIALS AND TAILPIECES.

IF MISS HAYES, MR. EVANS AND MR. SHAKESPEARE DID NOT EACH HAVE SUCH A FAITHFUL AND ABSORBED PUBLIC, MR. BOWLES MIGHT EASILY HAVE WALKED AWAY WITH "TWELFTH NIGHT." FOR THE PLAY IS, AFTER ALL, A COMEDY WITH MUSIC. IT HAS A MUSICAL BEGINNING AND A MUSICAL FINALE AND SONGS ALL THE WAY THROUGH.

NO ONE WRITING IN THE BROADWAY THEATER MAKES A SONG WITHIN A PLAY SO CHARMINGLY AS BOWLES DOES. HE DOES NOT AIM AT SONG HITS EASILY EXTRACTABLE FROM THEIR CONTEXT. HE AIMS RATHER TO CONCENTRATE A PLAY'S WHOLE MOOD AND PRESENTATION INTO BRIEF MUSICAL MOMENTS. HE AVOIDS ITALIANATE MELODIC PROPORTIONS. HIS SONGS COULD GO ON FOREVER, SO LITTLE HAVE THEY THE AIR OF GETTING ANYWHERE. THEY ARE AS STATIC AS DÉCOR, AS EXPRESSIVE AS GOOD COSTUMES.

EVERY MEMBER OF THE "TWELFTH NIGHT" CAST AND EVERY SCENE OF SHAKESPEARE'S PLAY WAS AIDED AND ENHANCED BY THE PRESENCE OF THIS SUMPTUOUS AND SUITABLE MUSIC, EVERY MEASURE OF IT EMBROIDERED BY HAND. AND WHEN THE WHOLE STAGE JOINED IN THE FINAL SONG IT WAS AS IF THE EVENING AND ITS APPLAUSE WERE BEING HANDED ON A PLATTER TO MR. BOWLES AS HOMAGE TO HIS SELF-EFFACING AND ACCURATE WORKMANSHIP IN THE PRECEDING SCENES.

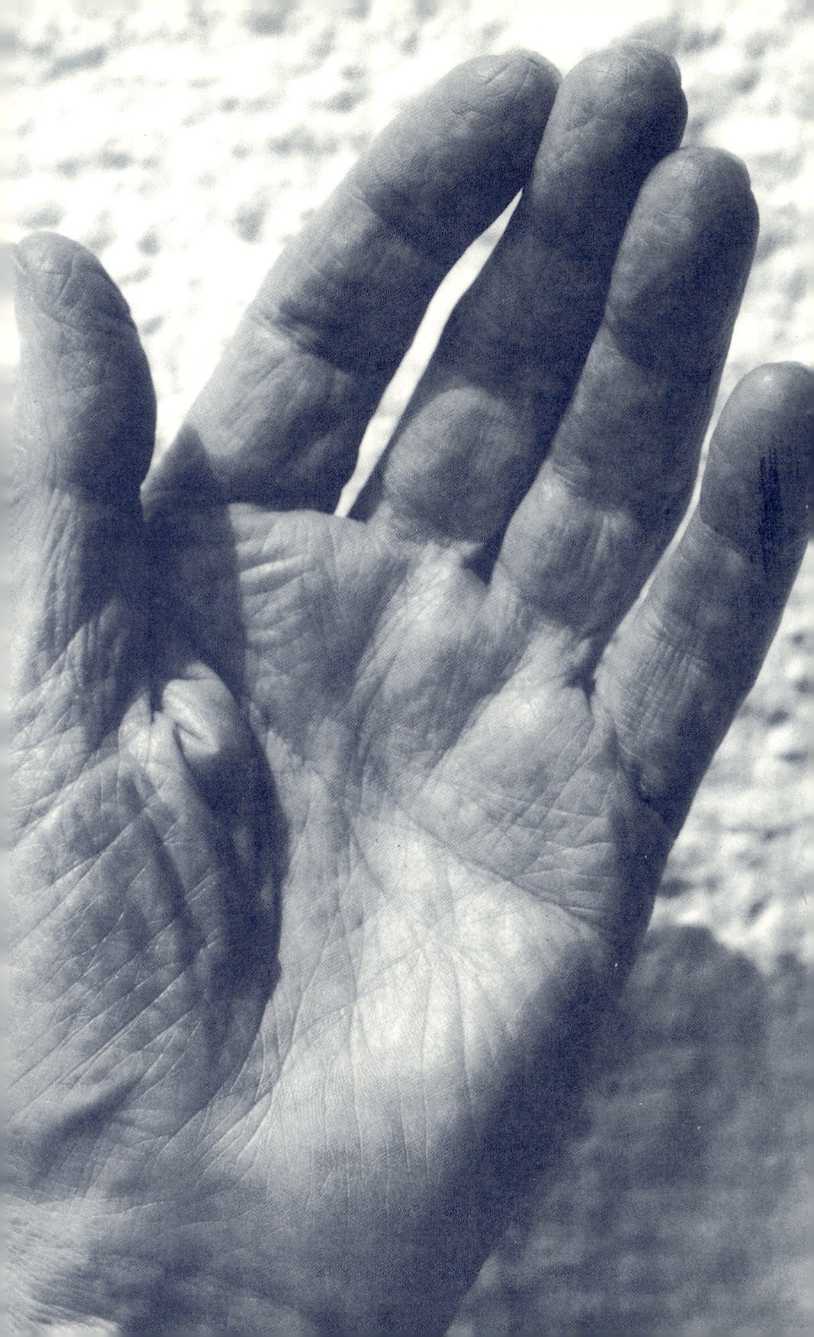

NEW BOWLES SCORE
GETS FIRST HEARING

"WIND REMAINS,"

A ZARZUELA OR SPANISH FORM OF MUSICAL THEATER, IS PRESENTED
AT MODERN ART MUSEUM

THIRD IN SERIES OF SERENADES
also FEATURES ARGENTINITA
and HER COMPANY

By HOWARD TAUBMAN

(The New York Times, 31 March 1943)

p.78 A NEW SCORE BY PAUL BOWLES, YOUNG AMERICAN COMPOSER, HAD ITS FIRST PERFORMANCE LAST NIGHT AT THE MUSEUM OF MODERN ART IN THE THIRD OF A SERIES OF FIVE SERENADES. THE MUSIC WAS FOR A ZARZUELA IN ONE ACT, "THE WIND REMAINS," WHICH THE COMPOSER ADAPTED FROM THE WORK OF GARCÍA LORCA, THE SPANISH POET.

A ZARZUELA IS A SPANISH FORM OF MUSICAL THEATER, COMBINING POPULAR AND SERIOUS MUSIC, DRAMA AND DANCE. "THE WIND REMAINS" COMBINED MUSIC, DRAMA AND DANCE, BUT TO THOSE UNFAMILIAR WITH THE TRADITION OF THE ZARZUELA IT MADE LITTLE OR NO SENSE. THE SPOKEN LINES WERE FILLED WITH STRANGE SYMBOLS, OFTEN APPARENTLY UNRELATED, AND NOW AND THEN THERE WERE PHRASES THAT COULD BE APPLIED TO WHAT WAS GOING ON BEHIND THE FOOTLIGHTS. AT ONE POINT A CHARACTER SAID TO ANOTHER, "WHAT ARE YOU SAYING? YOU TALK TOO MUCH."

EVALUATION OF SCORE: IT MAY BE THAT THE ZARZUELA CONVEYS SOMETHING TO THE SPANISH PEOPLE. LAST NIGHT "THE WIND REMAINS" WAS A SENSITIVE PLANT THAT COULD SCARCELY WITHSTAND TRANSPLANTING. IT WAS PRECIOUS MORE OFTEN THAN EXOTIC. BUT THAT DOES NOT DETRACT FROM THE QUALITY OF MR. BOWLES' MUSIC. IT HAD ATMOSPHERE; HIS WRITING FOR TENOR AND SOPRANO VOICE WAS SENSITIVE AND CONGENIAL; HIS SCORING FOR SMALL ORCHESTRA WAS ADROIT. HE IS A GIFTED THEATER COMPOSER.

"THE WIND REMAINS" WAS STAGED IN STYLIZED PRETENTIOUS AND VAPID FASHION BY SCHUYLER WATTS. THE SINGERS WERE ROMOLO DE SPIRITO, A GENEROUSLY ENDOWED TENOR, AND JEANNE STEPHENS, SOPRANO. THE DANCES WERE DIRECTED BY MERCE CUNNINGHAM, AND AMONG THE DANCERS WERE MR. CUNNINGHAM, JEAN ERDMAN, BARBARA BRAE, PAUL SWEENEY AND DAVID RAHER. MARIE MOTHERWELL, CLEMENT BRACE AND CLAUDE ALPHAND DID THE BEST THEY COULD WITH SPEAKING PARTS THAT SOUNDED AS IF GERTRUDE STEIN HAD HAD A HAND WITH THEM. THE SETTING WAS BY OLIVER SMITH AND THE COSTUMES BY KERMIT LOVE.

LEONARD BERNSTEIN CONDUCTS: LEONARD BERNSTEIN, TALENTED YOUNG AMERICAN CONDUCTOR, HANDLED THE BEHIND-THE-SCENES ORCHESTRA WITH SMOOTHNESS AND PRECISION. HE CONDUCTED A COLORFUL, METTLESOME PERFORMANCE OF "HOMAGE TO GARCÍA LORCA" BY THE LATE MEXICAN COMPOSER SILVESTRE REVUELTAS. HERE IS AN INDIVIDUAL SCORE, WITH HAUNTING THEMES, SAVAGE COLORS AND NATIVE RHYTHMS. THE MIDDLE MOVEMENT, A DIRGE IN MEMORY OF GARCÍA LORCA, WHO SPOKE FOR THE POPULAR FRONT DURING THE SPANISH CIVIL WAR AND WHO DIED MYSTERIOUSLY BEHIND THE FALANGIST LINES, HAD SEARCHING DIGNITY AND PATHOS.

THE EVENING ENDED WITH A BALLET BY ARGENTINITA, "EL CAFÉ DE CHINITAS," BASED ON A MALAGUENIAN FOLKSONG OF THE NINETEENTH CENTURY AS RECORDED BY GARCÍA LORCA. ARGENTINITA WAS ASSISTED BY HER COMPANY IN A PERFORMANCE THAT BROUGHT THE EVENING TO A SPIRITED END.

MUSIC

BY VIRGIL THOMSON

TWO B'S

(New York Herald Tribune, 6 March 1947)

THE COMPOSERS' FORUM, DIRECTED BY ASHLEY PETTIS, WAS REVIVED LAST NIGHT AT THE MUSEUM OF MODERN ART UNDER THE SPONSORSHIP OF THE NEW YORK PUBLIC LIBRARY'S MUSIC DIVISION. THE COMPOSERS WHOSE WORKS WERE EXPOSED, ATTACKED AND DEFENDED WERE PAUL BOWLES AND
p. 80 WILLIAM BERGSMA. A GREAT MANY EXCELLENT MUSICIANS TOOK PART, AND THE EXECUTIONS WERE GENERALLY ADMIRABLE. AT THE END OF THE CONCERT THERE WERE QUESTIONS, WHICH THE COMPOSERS ANSWERED, AND SOME SPONTANEOUS SPEAKING FROM THE FLOOR. THE MUSIC, HOWEVER, WAS FAR MORE LIVELY THAN THE DISCUSSION OF IT.

PAUL BOWLES, AT THIRTY-FOUR, IS AMERICA'S MOST ORIGINAL AND SKILLFUL COMPOSER OF CHAMBER MUSIC AND ONE OF THE MOST FECUND. HE WRITES CHIEFLY FOR UNEXPECTED AND DISPARATE COMBINATIONS OF INSTRUMENTS; AND HIS FORMAL STRUCTURE IS RARELY THAT OF CLASSICAL SONATA-FORM, THOUGH HE HAS NOT DISDAINED THIS FAMILIAR LAYOUT WHEN IT HAS SEEMED APPROPRIATE TO HIM. HE HAS INEXHAUSTIBLE MELODIC INVENTION, AN ENORMOUS FANCY IN INSTRUMENTAL FIGURATION, A DAINTY TASTE IN PRISMATIC HARMONY (AS IF

EACH CHORD WERE ACCOMPANIED BY ITS OWN REFRACTION) AND THE MOST SOPHISTICATED HAND FOR PERCUSSION NOW WORKING AMONG US. HIS EXPRESSIVE CONTENT IS NOSTALGIC AND EVOCATIVE OF THE VERNACULAR. SOMETIMES THE VERNACULAR IS MEXICAN, SOMETIMES SPANISH OR AFRICAN. AT ITS MOST POWERFUL, FOR AMERICANS, IT EVOKES THE AMERICAN URBAN MUSICAL IDIOM OF OUR CENTURY'S FIRST TWO DECADES.

PLAYING MASTERFULLY ON MELODIC REFERENCE, INGENIOUS ACCOMPANIMENT AND COLORISTIC VARIETY, RATHER [THAN] ON WEIGHT, HIS MUSIC PACKS NO EMOTIONAL WALLOPS; BUT ITS SENTIMENTAL FORCE IS ENORMOUS. ALSO, ITS INTELLECTUAL CONTENT IS OF THE MOST DISTINGUISHED. ITS EARLY MODEL WAS RAVEL, BUT THE COMPOSERS WHOSE WORK IT HAS MOST RESEMBLED IN LATE YEARS ARE ERIK SATIE AND SILVESTRE REVUELTAS. HE HAS LABORED LONG AND SUCCESSFULLY IN THE THEATER; THE SYMPHONY ORCHESTRA AND THE EDITORIAL VEIN OF CONTEMPORARY SYMPHONIC COMPOSERS ARE ALIEN TO HIS FASTIDIOUS TASTE AND PRECISE THOUGHT. LAST NIGHT'S RICHEST PIECE, WONDERFUL FOR ABUNDANT IMAGINATION AND FANCY OF EVERY KIND, WAS A SET OF SHORTISH NUMBERS CALLED "MUSIC FOR A FARCE," COMPOSED IN 1938 FOR A PROJECTED PRODUCTION BY ORSON WELLES OF WILLIAM GILLETTE'S "TOO MUCH JOHNSON."

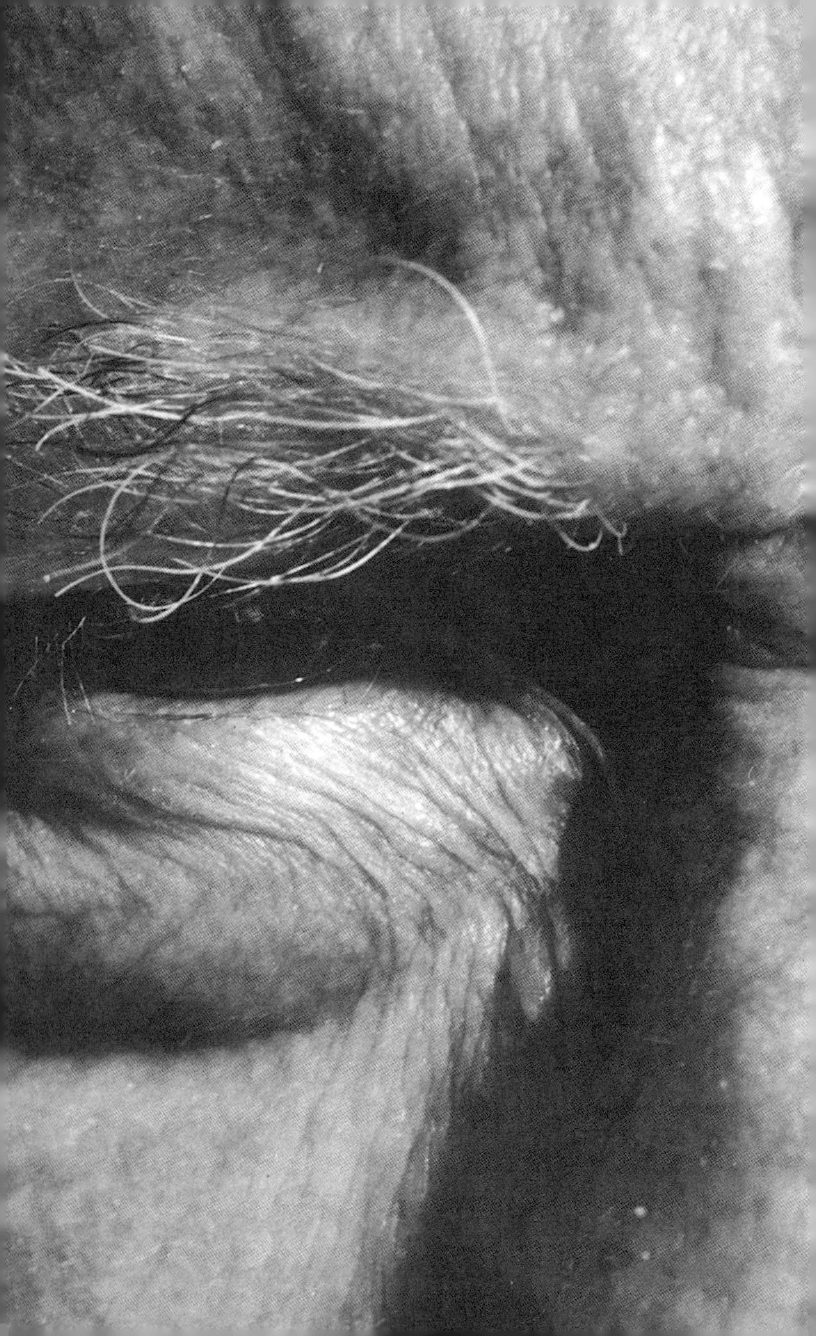

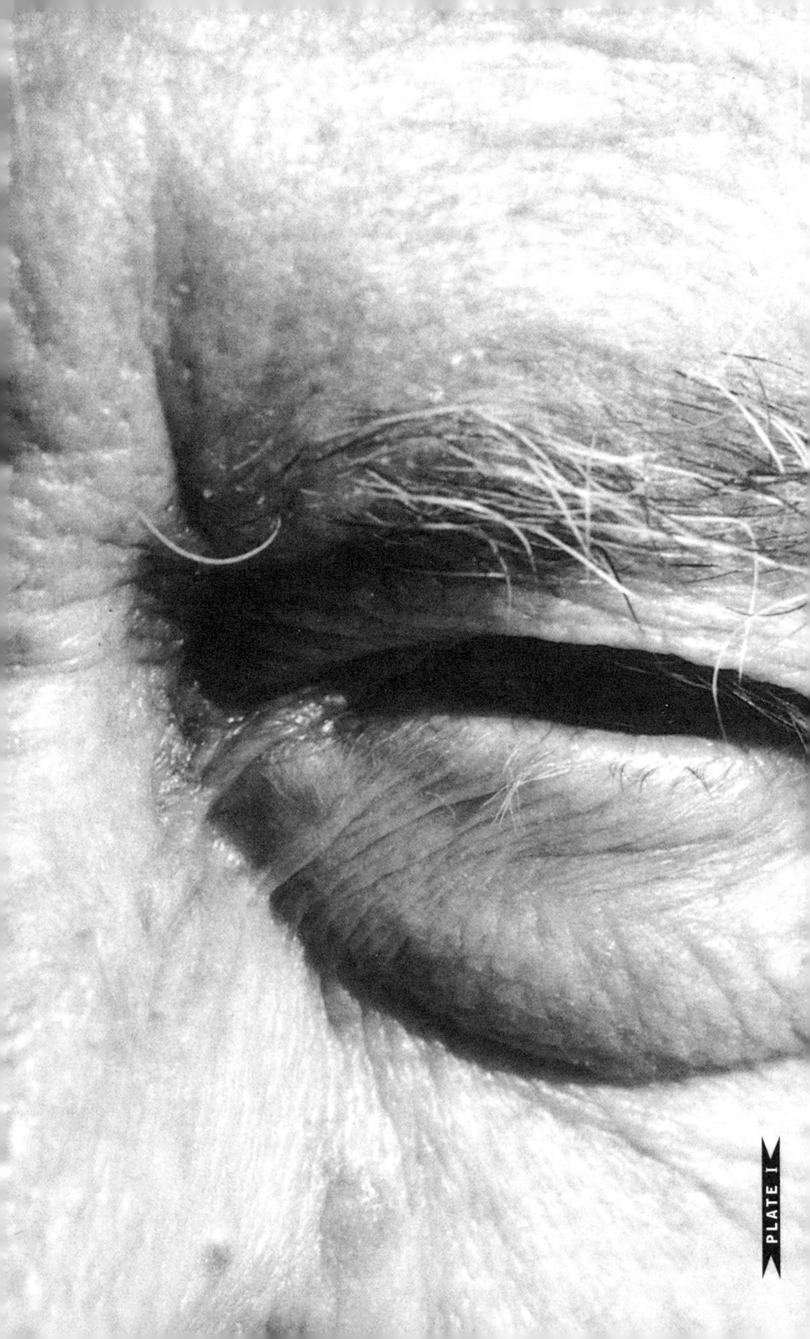

PLATE I

PLATE II

PLATE III

PLATE IV

Fernruf 62
Dessauer Straßenbahn
Kraft-Omnibus-Verkehr
25 Pf
24181
16867
AUTES HÄNDEKLATSCHEN
OORLOG A.
ZIJ DIE BIJ DE 10-JARK
MOBILISATIE VAN HU
WILLEN BLIJK GEVEN B
Friedr. Baum
Fabrikanten feiner
bekannt, sind aus dem
eschmiedet, sorgfältig
9
Kurt Schwitters 1930
Oorlog

PLATE V

PLATE VI

KLEINE DADA SOIRÉE

PICABIA
J'ENFILE MES BOTTINES
TOUS LES MATINS

PROGRAMMA

HAAG SCH 1923

K.K.

BINNENHOF 8

DADASOFIE THÉO

INLEIDING DOOR THÉO VAN DOESBURG

GROSSEN GLORREICHEN REVOLUTION IN REVON DOOR KURT SCHWITTERS

DADA EST CONTRE
LE FUTUR
DADA EST MORT
DADA EST IDIOT, VIVE
DADA ! DADA
DADA N'EST PAS
UNE ÉCOLE LITTÉ-
RAIRE HURLE
TRISTAN TZARA

BEI RHEUMATISCHEN
ZAHNENSCHMERZEN
UND KOPFWEH GENÜGEN MEIST
2-3 REVONTABLETTEN UND ZWAR
AUFTAN BRUCH

GEPACTZE GEDICHTE VON ABSTRACTER LYRIK BIS ZUM URLAUT DOOR KURT SCHWITTERS

DADA EXISTE DEPUIS
TOUJOURS LA SAINTE
VIERGE DÉJÀ FUT
DADAISTE

BANALITÄTEN

UND ALS SIE IN DIE TÜTE SAH
DA WAREN ROTE KIRSCHEN DRIN
DA MACHTE SIE DIE TÜTE ZU
DA WAR DIE TÜTE ZU.

ERIC SATIE'S
RAG-TIME-DADA

SIMULTANEÏSTISCH-MECHAN: DANS DOOR HUSZAR

TREMARCIE PEF LA BESTIE VAN PIETI KLAVIER

PLATE VII

Sinfonia
Ouverture
Eugene Berman
Designs
for
Igor Stravinsky
1942–1972
by Igor Stravinsky

PLATE VIII

PLATE IX

—avoir l'apprenti dans le soleil.—

Marcel Duchamp. 1914.

PLATE X

PLATE XI

PLATE XII

PAUL BOWLES

(1 November 1949)

THE SEASON OF PROMISE

BY

PEGGY GLANVILLE-HICKS

IT WAS PLANNED THAT THIS PIECE SHOULD BE CALLED The Daring Young Man on the Esthetic Trapeze—THAT IT SHOULD BE AS GAY AND FULL OF ESPRIT AS THE COMPOSER AND HIS MUSIC OFTEN ARE; YET ON REFLECTION THE STORY SEEMED SOLEMN, NOT ONLY IN ITS RELATION TO PAUL BOWLES, BUT BECAUSE HIS CASE IS NOT UNIQUE, AND HIS CRISIS IS ONE THAT WILL CONFRONT MANY ANOTHER YOUNG ARTIST IN OUR TIME.

Paul Bowles is one of the most uncategorical composers in the American scene. He represents an enigma to many, is a negligible figure to others, and to some p.103
few—this writer among them—one of the rarer musical minds, and potentially an extraordinary composer.

Well known though he is to both commercial and concert worlds, Broadway does not claim him as a servant of Mammon, and the long-haired boys, dubious of the esthetic tightrope that he walks, hesitate to welcome him in as a servant of God. A solitary, gifted poet in both words and music, Bowles wanders like a philosopher with his stone in the wilderness that exists between the polarity points of economics and artistic values.

His problem was twofold, involving both material and metaphysical planes (as an artist's problems are apt to do) and the balance between the two: Musically, it was to find a synthesis, new and strong and uniquely his own, of the assortment of curious musical ingredients he had assembled from folk sources, both primitive and urban. Materially, the problem was to earn a living while functioning as himself, and without infringement of his artistic integrity. To a large extent he solved the material problem, and to a large extent he still fails to solve the far more complex and all-demanding musical one.

On the material level, Bowles early discovered two profitable outlets for his talents in music and letters. In letters, he worked for some years as a critic on the staff of the New York *Herald Tribune*, and came to be known and respected as a man of judgment, taste and wit. He wrote lucidly and with musical insight; and it was a job that kept him in touch with contemporary musical trends of all kinds, and also supplied a far wider knowledge of classical repertory than formal music study usually provides. In the world of fiction too he has shown an intermittent interest since his teen-age debut in the pages of the Paris *transition*, and his gift for
p. 104 short stories has gained him something of a reputation as a writer.

As a musician he functioned from WPA days onward, in the theater as a composer of incidental music, a genre in which he set a high standard and in which he became not only the most sought-after but the most highly paid writer. His rare sense of atmospheres, and an ability to create vivid moods with brief fragmentary musical interludes made his theater scores real chamber music of a quality unique in the commercial world; for though he would make many a concession on technical grounds, at no point would he ever make any on esthetic grounds. Even the tones of an occasional electronic organ or similar artistic hazard forced upon him by the house would be disciplined in his scores with an objectivity that changed its whole character. His resourcefulness in gaining his musical ends within theatrical restrictions was always remarkable, and amply bore out his own contention that any sounds, from a telephone bell to an oboe, could be the materials of art.

It has often been said that a serious composer cannot function on Broadway and in the commercials fields without an ultimate loss of quality or integrity. It has also been countered that it is not so much the work itself that brings about a deterioration, but the life one leads to get it, and to keep on getting it in sufficient quantities to live thereby. In truth, neither the work nor the way of life will necessarily harm the composer if he retains a sense of artistic direction, an aim and conviction held firmly within the heart so that all activities are simply a means to that end. It is possible (as we will later consider) that certain delayed psychological repercussions result when too much of an artist's creative energy is diverted into commercial channels; but from a purely technical and esthetic standpoint it p. 105 would seem that a young composer can be active in all the functional outlets of his day, and that he can do so, as Bowles has demonstrated, without impairing his musical standards in any way. If a composer established as a man of achievement in the serious musical field chooses to earn his living on Broadway it need do him no harm, and can bring a fresh vitality into the commercial forum.

Let him start getting his values mixed, however, or lose his sense of direction so that means and ends become reversed, so that—professional allegiances forgotten—the prestige bestowed by the art world is used to gain entrance into the commercial one, and he will become the victim of a disease he will find difficult to check. An indefinable change will take place, and the men of good faith in the art and profession, suspicious that their endorsement is being misused, will veer away and endorse no more, and the trapeze act between the kingdoms of God and Mammon becomes not only an esthetic but an ethical one as well.

In the commercial field, the basic difference between the artist-composer and the commercial composer is simply that, given a clash between gain and values, the commercial man chooses gain, the artist chooses values. If it has seemed to some of his colleagues that Bowles was playing both ends against the middle, or that there was some doubt as to which was the means to what end, the real direction of his aim will ultimately be proven by the degree and kind of his serious output in music. The detrimental effects, if any, of his long exposure to the ways of the commercial world will also become apparent in this sphere.

In composition, his point of departure and train of thought have from the outset been radically
p.106 different from anyone else's, in that he has sought a pattern of construction and a type of unrhetorical, unclimactic music that has no real European prototype. Apprenticeships to Aaron Copland and, later, to Virgil Thomson were the extent of his formal studies, and his original if limited technical adroitness has been learned in action, mainly in the theater, where he also evolved a varied, stringent and very personal manner of chamber orchestration.

Because of his resistance to academic study, Bowles is regarded by some as an amateur. In one sense this is true; for the amateur, in common with the greatest originator (the one transcending his ignorance and the other his knowledge) accepts the challenge to create directly from within himself, leaning on no pre-conceived systems or criteria. Bowles' lack of interest in orthodoxy came not from any inability to learn, for he possesses a brilliant brain, but from a realization that almost nothing in accepted writing methods applied organically or instrumentally to what he heard in his mind's ear as his own music.

If Copland taught him anything it never showed in his music. But his debt to Thomson is considerable, and in his earlier works very evident. His finesse in prosody bears testimony to the guidance of a master in this art, and contributes greatly to Bowles' special success in the song form. But above all he learned from Thomson not a technical, so much as an ideological, method of procedure—the Dada idea of Erik Satie. In this respect he is Thomson's truest disciple, just as Thomson is today Satie's truest disciple.

This procedure, a method whereby styles, period mannerisms, all kinds of musical elements alien to one's own style, can be contained within that style, was a usable device, and as such, instantly absorbed by Bowles. It enabled him to give at least the coherence of a pastiche variety to the seemingly irreconcilable musical ingredients that appealed to p.107
him; these ranged from the honky-tonk pianola style and jazz esthetic through the milk-bottle, cigar-box, factory-whistle phase of "noise-track" Dada to the subtleties, both melodic and rhythmic, of the Mexican, Peruvian, Afro-Hispanic folk music that he loved to collect.

Certain of his works—*Scènes d'Anabase* (1932); the *Cantata* (1933) for soprano, male quartet, harmonium and percussion; the chamber orchestra piece *Music for a Farce* (1938)—demonstrate an aspect of the pastiche form that he evolved. In the case of the *Cantata* the whole piece is evocative of a musical "manner," while in *Music for a Farce* the jazz esthetic is alluded to, not to say quoted within the bounds of a concert piece, each detail of the jazz formula being present, from the reiterative bass to the melodic and harmonic clichés. In *Scènes d'Anabase* (to texts of St. John Perse) one finds melodic fragments of pure Arabic line and detail incorporated with skill into a French-style neo-classic shape and context. The choice of ensemble here (oboe, tenor and piano) is particularly suited in its rather nasal timbre to the whole atmosphere of the work and makes it one of the composer's most effective pieces in the collage category of the earlier crop of works.

> In his search for the form inherent in his materials, Bowles' style undergoes a series of mutations. When he works with an idea based on a primitive subject matter—Central American, African—the raw material is a direct human statement, aural in manifestation, not even systematized to the point of notation, but packed full of vital emotional content. It is much further from our musical vocabulary than is the jazz or popular material, for instance, for its timbres and intervals are unreproducible in any exactness at all, and the rhythms are
> p. 108 far more subtle than most European ears can detect, let alone notate.

Thus, the effort of listening, of concentration, of sheer creative force brought to bear to extract from such music its natural essence and re-give it in a new statement is a truly creative process—achieved emotionally, both in absorbing the impulse from the primitive sounds and in imparting to it a contemporary expression. The emotional ingredient in art, as in life, is the cement that makes of component parts a unified whole, and Bowles' musical experiment (though he is not the only one to work along these lines) is highly impressive.

In relation to this process, two instances are notable. In his score for the Belgian government film, *Congo*, he writes several intensely rhythmic sections (quantitative rather than cumulative in tension scheme) which maintain a state of being (as primitive music does) and do not build climaxes except in the psychological hypnotic sense. The sections in question are built closely on actual African rhythm and texture patterns, and, apart from marimbas and a few extraneous and exotic percussion elements that Bowles habitually uses, the instrumentation and notation is that of any normal orchestral layout. Percussion is extensive, and subtle, yet the impact of the music comes from the music itself, not from any added percussive trimmings. It is integral in the composition and does not rely on presentation devices; it is built from the very nature of the material used, and produces upon the listener precisely the effect of the African music to which it is an expressive counterpart.

This score, written in 1944, was perhaps the first instance of real synthesis as opposed to collage in Bowles' work; and although the composer was aware of the difference (he carried the process to an amazing degree of abstraction in the finale of his *Sonata for Two Pianos* [1946]), he did not appear to have p.109
realized what it was that could cause synthesis and fusion in one case, and collage or pastiche in another.

From the activity of the intellect alone, one gets pastiche—a welding that gives a new look to old ideas. From the activity of emotion (the unspecific emotion of art), from an impact deeply experienced and re-given to artistic utterance, one gets fusion, synthesis, a new type, a prototype. The mind is a conductor, a vessel, not an originator; art that proceeds from the mind alone is invariably sterile. The heart is the sifter, the integrator; it works slowly, and its white-hot concentration alone can transform raw material into art, the base metal of sound into the pure gold of music.

When Bowles uses the jazz esthetic, the material employed is material that has already passed through a mentalization process. Certainly jazz stems from Africa, just as the primitive material under discussion does, and in its improvisational versions, such as the jam session, it retains much of its native vitality, be it somewhat dope-dimmed and despairing. But by the time jazz reaches the ten-inch disc and the public, it is the ultimate in cliché, its exact form and length, its harmony, its melodic type being one of the most notable examples of the freezing process of mentalization. It is already crystallized and can only be used by the composer as decorative matter, superimposed on a formal unit that stems from another tradition (that of classical music) and not from its own nature as material. It is forever an arrangement; even its moods are borrowed moods, the nostalgia of reference.

In between the two stools—Africa straight and Africa Broadway—Bowles falls with something of a bang, and only sometimes, by instinct, does he get on his feet again. He tries and tries to mix the two Africas, thereby delaying indefinitely the formation of a structural method that would enable him to
p.110 make a form of his idiom, to really compose and create the exciting and varied rhythmic scores that he has always heard in his mind's ear.

Another trap awaited him, and he fell into that one too. This was the problem of slow movements, those idyllic, lyrical, passionate or intense (according to bent) sections in a composer's work that are so often the measure of his real quality in that they reveal the expressive degree. How to make his slow movements match esthetically his quick ones: this was a critical point, and it is one that has perplexed many a modern composer. In the neo-classic school the slow movement has often been stylized almost out of existence into a desiccated, heartless little trifle that separates two snappy allegros; while in the atonal group it is often stretched out in agonized threads to a veritable wailing-wall of dissonantly oblique angles. For Bowles, whose earliest musical manifestation was a most beautiful and touching melodic gift, the impasse was critical, since his expressive impulse was unable to speak fully through the technical resources that he had formulated.

In using the jazz esthetic he found that the only kind of slow movement that seemed to belong was a pastiche version of a blues or some similar borrowed convention from the jazz custom, currently associated with the categories from which he took his brisker material.

Similarly, when he used real Africana (not literally, since this music is aural, providing an emotional starting point, not a thematic one) he found no pattern at hand in Africana that could serve as a blueprint for slow movements, and so he turned to the wistful, evasive mood of sentimentality in the vaguely French manner that has become more and more the substance of his adagios.

The *Sonata for Two Pianos* is an excellent example of the mixed esthetics resulting from this confusion. It is a fine piece, however, an important point in Bowles' evolution, and is still perhaps the most p.111
important concert piece he has written, notwithstanding the more ambitious *Concerto for Two Pianos and Chamber Orchestra* of a year or two later.

The sonata sums up three phases of his writing. The neo-classicism (both technical and esthetic) of the first movement is the most organized point he has reached in terms of technical maturity and the meeting of ends and means; the ideas are good, plain, and used to the full with resource, vim and taste. It is a summation of a style he played with in the *Piano Sonatina* (1932-33) and in the *Flute Sonata* (1932), not without mishap. The slow movement is not free of sentimentality, but the tendency to harmonic cliché is an undertone, not an actuality. The finale, though esthetically the most out of place, is the most exciting piece of writing, and represents an abstraction drawn from his experiments in rhythm as form. Thematic and melodic elements are totally absent, giving precedence to an amazing complexity of rhythm layers intoned in harmonic handfuls of notes, used purely percussively, so dissonant as to be meaningless harmonically. Its structural principle is its rhythm texture, its form is its length.

These three movements are extremely disparate, yet the work holds conviction, a greater conviction than the concerto which was written next. The reason seems to be that each of the three movements of the sonata is derived from a type of material, be it classical or primitive, that will bear creative development, whereas the concerto again harks back to the jazz esthetic, an immutable substance, and the result is less a fused and creative result, more a pastiche, a re-arrangement—a surrealism where fragments are stirred into a new relationship, but where each fragment is still glaringly what it was, recalling former juxtapositions.

This is a harsh verdict on an intangible failure. Actually the concerto is, to all intents and purposes, a highly successful, not to say brilliant
p.112 work. It is the most extended piece of concert writing that Bowles has achieved, and formally the most unified. The brief scherzo movement is one of the best pieces of pure music heard in recent seasons. But apart from the scherzo, the work contains too many compromises with cheapness, with remnants from his past (the most superficial remnants), from every phase of his writing back to the Dada one of the telephone bells, milk bottles, cigar boxes—externalizations of the "surprise tactic" that are utterly redundant when a composer has surprise elements galore organically inherent in his materials if he chooses well and uses properly. It is indubitably true of all art from architecture to music, that the form and design must follow the principle upon which one builds. Anything else produces a "horseless carriage" structure, no matter how shiny and attractive.

If Bowles' chief problem and only salvation is to

achieve synthesis, the concerto is a retrogressive, not a progressive, step from the sonata. It has achieved formal and stylistic unity by returning to an esthetic capable only of pastiche, of a mental discipline that, chic and distinctive though it is, is an artistic compromise for all that.

Why should so gifted and intelligent a man have not as yet been able to formulate from a veritable gold mine of musical nuggets a convincing and personally expressive idiom?

It has sometimes been suggested that he is quite satisfied with the exotic hybrid that he has already produced; and certainly his degree of public success and recognition is considerable, although it is accorded not so much by the serious musical world and his own colleagues as by a personal following of Broadway culture-hounds, entranced to see their esthetic stepping out in Paris clothes, and younger middle-brows, who sense some proletarian synthesis p. 113
of vernacular and aristocratic assets. But Bowles himself will readily admit that his aim—a different psychological basis, and a non-occidental concept of structure—is probably disastrous for him as far as a career in the usual sense is concerned, and that the closer he gets to his objective the less will he be correctly understood in either of his spheres of operation.

Bowles has perhaps in part explained the delay in stabilizing a method when he avers that his intermittent sorties into the wage-earning world, to cover a concert, or to hastily concoct a score for a Broadway show, disrupt the poise of concentration on his own trend of thought, so that the time and leisure left over from such activities, extensive though it is, is scarcely usable for serious creative work. The shutting out of other sounds, the maintaining within himself of the state of isolation, mentally and emotionally, in which he contacts his own point of focus is scarcely begun when it is again interrupted. And so by constantly deferring the real issue (the need to bring his intellectual resources and technical data in line with, and subjugated to his deepest expressive needs) he finds it increasingly hard to face the magnitude of the creative, integrative effort and will necessary to remake the mental-emotional fusion.

When he is obliged to write, he writes with his intellect alone, from his knowledge and experience, from his technical fluency in an idiom that does not contain his deeper expression, since it was evolved without the inclusion of that degree. Having mastered the art of writing to order for money, without making damaging esthetic concessions, he found himself in a strange psychological dilemma—unable, in the leisure thus gained, to write at all without the artificial stimulus of a fee.

The problem of superficial production is
one of the more serious ones in the arts today. It
p.114 results in a great deal of shallow art, and—what is
much more serious—a despair and impotence in the
artists themselves that comes from unfulfillment.

Among the several causes the educational and economic environments seem dominant, though a kind of personal disintegration is also deeply involved. The artist discovers early that the race goes to the swift; that the prizes, the awards, the scholarships, performances, publications, recordings, even the pick of the jobs, all go to the ones who can produce fastest, who turn out the slickest, most packaged and standardized product, typed to the author's label and reliably undeviating from his established "line."

To compete in the race, the artist must travel at the speed that only the brain can travel. He cannot afford to await that slower process of integrated creative evolution that the mind, emotional degree and personal growth together can produce, and that alone would be an adequate and satisfying creative expression to himself.

There is far too much thought about the technical aspects of music, the aspects subject to analysis; and there is far too little known or thought about the psychological, emotional, spiritual states of the artist, whose great force comes from his need and ability to achieve and maintain a state of contact with his inspiration, a state produced by an unspecific emotional mood which is the wave length whereon he contacts his own point of integration.

The maintaining of this point of contact is a power that is to him a technique—his real technique—a technique to be served by the secondary technique of craftsmanship. It is a power of inner listening that requires meditation, and that increases with cultivation, like the power to love, and which, similarly, can wither and die by neglect.

When it fails, there is an individual tragedy, and the sense of failure that results, in even the most
(apparently) successful writer, composer, novelist, or p. 115
playwright, is a saddening thing to see; for with the transforming element of feeling atrophied, and with the sole weapon of mind (that can transcend nothing), he becomes either a "one book man" or begins to go around in circles, reiterating, resurfacing, transposing the same old themes until they become a meaningless collection of relics.

He begins to run ideologically and geographically from himself, from an inexplicable sterility. He loses the power to feel simply and profoundly the simple and profound things. Originality becomes not a surpassing in stature, but a deviation—any deviation from the norm.

He runs and runs, but whether he runs to Italy, to the Sahara, to an analyst or into personal disasters that constantly disrupt reflection and postpone facing the need for regeneration; whether he takes to drink, to the nihilism of Sartre, to the cult of agony where the mind continues to assassinate the life of the heart—it is the same story. He runs from the ultimate responsibility of becoming himself in the pattern of his potentialities, and of realizing an art that is expressive of fulfillment, not of frustration.

He is like one of the blind-folded well-donkeys of Spain, who, the ever-repeating landscape shut from view, trot patiently on, forever drawing water, forever sustained by the hallucination of progress that movement without vision brings.

Two years ago Paul Bowles uprooted himself from New York's musical community and from his enviably lucrative niche in the theater and journalistic worlds, and left for North Africa, following a long-set pattern of intermittent wandering and retracing his own footsteps of fifteen and twenty years ago. Whether he too is following a pattern of escape, or has retired to the wilderness to "face the music" will
p. 116 be proven by the work that will come forth.

In Morocco, and with journeys into the Sahara, he has been living surrounded by music of a type most near to his ideal and most dear to his heart. It is the music of the Andalous, an ancient Afro-Hispanic style that is tonal in equilibrium, with an exquisite melodic development and an infinite polyrhythmic subtlety that should provide him with the ideal environment in which to grow to musical maturity.

During the years of absence, however, he has not so far produced any music, though he has been active in the literary field. It is possibly either that he has felt the need to simplify his problem (for the technique of words involves many fewer layers of complexity than does that of sound), or that his state of mind called for a more liberal definition of it.

Strangely enough, in reading the recently published novel, *The Sheltering Sky*, and the many short stories that have come out of this period, one becomes aware of the presence of both the qualities and the lacks that are manifest in his music. The terms of expression and the ideas are exquisite in their selectivity, and the material is exotic, unusual, poetically brilliant fragment by fragment; but in the books, as in the music, there is again absent some emotional degree that would weld the vivid components into a meaningful whole. The themes, moreover, are almost without exception those of frustration, guilt, humiliation—the classic themes of unfulfillment; and it is clear that whatever the psychological impasse may be that has delayed the synthesis and integration in his music, there is a parallel visible in the books.

The season of promise is already unduly prolonged, for Bowles is not a young composer. But at forty he is not yet an old one, and if he can make of his exotic retreat not an escape from his personal challenges, but a vital workshop wherein to contact p. 117
the original resources of his own nature, he may yet come forth with as rich an expression as any we have encountered in contemporary music.

His gifts are great, but his problems have always been, and remain, far more subtle and complex than those of the composer who finds himself technically and psychologically content and in sympathy with ready-made schools of thought. If he is able to penetrate to the inner nature of his own impulse and discover the psychological and structural principle upon which he should build, he will emerge with a new and moving art form.

"Several seasons ago, when I was in Tangier, and speaking to Paul Bowles about performances of my opera, The Ghosts of Versailles, he asked, 'What's Lincoln Center?'"

JOHN CORIGLIANO

"Paul Bowles is the composer of some of my favorite American music."

STEPHEN SONDHEIM

p. 118

"Paul Bowles is the only man who looks comfortable in Morocco wearing a suit. He's also the one who invites the most magic (especially at dinner) and the least likely to admit it. I love him for that and let's just say, for the sake of brevity, a lot more."

DEBRA WINGER

"I was always impressed by his original mind..."

LUKAS FOSS

The Songs of Paul Bowles

by Ben Yarmolinsky

"An artist chooses his subjects; that is his way of praising"
— Friedrich Nietzsche[1]

Paul Bowles' songs refuse the distinction between art song and popular song. They are cosmopolitan both in their wide range of musical idioms, and in their choice of languages—English, French and Spanish. They are mostly quite brief—rarely more than two minutes long, and often closer to a single minute. With the exception of a few songs written for the theater, they were neither commissioned nor written for particular occasions. They represent the composer's free choice of both text and musical style.

Bowles' attitude toward singing is characteristically idiosyncratic. He professes a distaste for the classically trained Western voice, and even claims to dislike vocal music in general. (His mentor Aaron Copland was of the same opinion.) Strange for a man with such literary tastes; stranger still for a composer at least half of whose *oeuvre* consists of vocal music.

"the lyrics wouldn't exist at all if it weren't for the fact that we live in a society where instrumental music is irrelevant"
— Frank Zappa[2]

"Words are words and music is music," according to Bowles.[3] If, as he wrote, "The writing of music is, of course, a communion with the unknown, nothing more,"[4] then the writing of music with words mediates that communion. No matter what the style, the melding of word and tone removes song from the realm of pure music. Certainly, the incommensurability of music with language is one of its most important features. Mendelssohn believed that the meaning of music was too specific for words; Schoenberg dreaded

(1)
Friedrich Nietzsche, *The Gay Science* (New York, 1974), trans. Walter Kaufmann, vol. III, p. 245.

(2)
As quoted in the New York *Times, Book Review*, Sunday, 11 June 1995.

(3)
Paul Bowles, conversation with author, May 1994.

(4)
Paul Bowles to Peggy Glanville-Hicks, 16 January 1948, *In Touch: The Letters of Paul Bowles*, ed. Jeffrey Miller (New York, 1994) (hereinafter *IT*), p. 188.

the day when music would be psychoanalyzed and its meanings parsed; Stravinsky insisted that music was nothing more than abstract patterns of sound. The point in every case is the same, that music should be heard for itself, not as a vehicle for a message that can be expressed in words. When a piece of music has lyrics, its musical values are more susceptible to being ignored.

Bowles' attitude toward song is analogous to Marianne Moore's toward poetry:

I too dislike it.
Reading it, however, with a perfect contempt for it, one discovers in it after all, a place for the genuine.[5]

(5)
The Complete Poems of Marianne Moore (New York, 1982), "Poetry," p. 36.

What constitutes the genuine in song? For Bowles, as for many other twentieth-century composers, the answer was to be found in folk and popular music. A multi-culturalist *avant la lettre*, by his mid-twenties he had had ample exposure to non-Western vocal music, not to mention

p. 120

the folk-derived experiments of Bartók and early Stravinsky. Bowles knew empirically how "unnatural" or at least how uncommon the sound of the European *bel canto* is among the singing styles of the world.

Art-music will get what it needs not from new subjects to sing about (i.e., the proletariat or a hundred other literary ideas), nor from technical devices (quarter tones and careful rhythms, etc., as such), but from new ways to sing, which means that it will be increasingly conscious of folk-musics of all corners of the globe, particularly the now unfamiliar corners. The Italian idea will be but one among scores of others....

When one considers the potentialities of endless variety lying latent in the human throat, and hears the miserable and pitiful sounds which issue from a concert hall during a famous singer's recital, one commences to realize the size of the task that lies ahead of the composer and the truly creative interpreter to keep this form of music [art song] alive beyond the time of the present dying generation. Because the next generation won't take it.[6]

(6)
To William Treat Upton, spring 1935, *IT*, pp. 158-159.

I haven't heard a concert since last February. I think Duke Ellington is really the best source of inspiration. And La Niña de los Peines with Niño Richard.[7]

Bowles' song aesthetic is grounded in the notion that lyric expression must appear to be natural. The idea of natural lyric expression is best exemplified by folk and popular singers, whose unselfconscious vocal production serves as a model of what singing should be—the human equivalent of birdsong. The aesthetic is consistent: against the rhythmic flabbiness of a Straussian orchestra, the precision and swing of Duke Ellington's band; against the screeching of a Kirsten Flagstad singing Wagner, La Niña de los Peines singing the intricately ornamented *cante jondo* of flamenco; against the deadly boredom of a subscription concert at the symphony, an open-air *ahouache* of the High Atlas in which an entire village actively participates in both music and dance. Already in the 1930s, Bowles had staked out an aesthetic position that he has maintained ever since.

(7)
Paul Bowles to Aaron Copland, November 1932, *IT*, p. 106.

Then, as now, his was not a position with which everyone agreed. Elliott Carter maintained that Bowles' music deprives folk music of its meaning. There is a grain of truth in this criticism. There were then (as there are today) composers whose appropriation of folk and popular materials amounts to an exploitative musical tourism. Bowles' approach was more nuanced; in his music the primary musical materials are filtered through an individual sensibility and transformed into a personal statement. (Of course, some of these transformations are more complex than others. A song like *Heavenly Grass* utterly transcends its folksong model. Some of the Latin American piano pieces seem to be little more than arrangements of local tunes.)

The overproduction of ersatz folk music and "arrangements" of folk materials was symptomatic of the musical populism of the Depression and war years. Folk music was identified with the political left and the anti-Fascist movement, and appreciated more for its ideological symbolism than for its musical values. The folk music movement became confused with a sort of cultural nationalism. Naturally, as a composer Bowles rebelled against this antimusical attitude. In August 1939, he wrote to Charles-Henri Ford, "I have been setting folk music for months. *Assez*."[8] He excluded the settings of twelve American folk songs he produced for the WPA Music Project from his 1984 *Selected Songs* on the grounds that he had done them for the money. As a cosmopolitan admirer of everything from Berber music to the blues, Bowles must have found it hard to muster enthusiasm for the exaltation of the Anglo-American folk song. Perhaps more important, Aaron Copland had pretty well cornered the market for musical Americana.

(8)
IT, p. 165.

p. 122

For all of his disdain of Western European musical ideals of vocal tone, Bowles' songs are written for that most Western European combination of voice and piano. And although the songs don't generally call for extremes of range or of technical dexterity, they demand a well-trained voice. The vocal lines are eminently singable, in natural phrase lengths, and move mostly step-wise with occasional well-prepared leaps. There is almost no melismatic writing—the policy is generally one note per syllable. The question is an aesthetic rather than a technical one: how to create an illusion of utter naturalness and ease in singing? This is a difficult problem, and one not limited to our time; even Brahms wrote songs that aspired to the artlessness of folk song.

Like many songs by Kurt Weill, Francis Poulenc, and Manuel DaFalla, Bowles' songs may be delivered more effectively by a cabaret singer than by a song recitalist. Cabaret singers understand song as theater, and Bowles' songs work as little pieces of theater. It is worth remembering that Bowles made his living as a theater composer. Richard Hundley, a contemporary songwriter in the Bowles tradition, characterizes Bowles as "pre-Sondheim." Like Sondheim, Bowles conceived of a song as a little one-act play. Some of his songs, among them *Song of an Old Woman* (also known as *Farther from the Heart*) on a Jane Bowles lyric, were originally performed as cabaret numbers.

The texts of Bowles' songs—by authors ranging from Charles-Henri Ford, Federico García Lorca, and Tennessee Williams, to Jane Bowles, Gertrude Stein, and St. John Perse—are unified only by their brevity and concision, with a bias toward authors known by the composer. The poems tend to be in simple verse forms analogous to the simple song forms in which they are cast. García Lorca was a collector of Spanish folk songs himself and many of his poems are modelled on the verses he collected. Likewise, Tennessee Williams based his *Blue Mountain Ballads* on the idiom of the Southern poor, and Charles-Henri Ford attempted to capture the idiom of Southern blacks in his libretto for the lost opera *Denmark Vesey*. But these are "high" art songs too. When the texts are literary, they are very literary. When they are patterned on "low" art models, the quality of the texts is consistently several cuts above that of the folk or popular models on which they are based.

The song forms Bowles employs are mostly of the garden variety: the musical theater AABA form, the strophic folk ballad form, and the classic *da capo* ABA form, often with a varied recapitulation. There are few instances of a completely through-composed setting; even the songs that have no formal repetitions are usually unified by a repeating accompaniment figure. The harmonic vocabulary of the songs is, in the words of Virgil Thomson, "a seventh-chord harmony which more composers than this one have learned out of Ravel."[9] It is personalized by

(9)
Preface, *Selected Songs by Paul Bowles* (Santa Fe, 1984).

unexpected modulations, and rich piano scoring. No expressionist, Bowles provides a sonorous backdrop for the text, articulates its structure, and enhances its natural curves with a melodic line that never calls attention to itself. His accompaniments rarely paint the text directly; rather, they set a mood or atmosphere. Only a few of the songs could survive as melodies sung without accompaniment. Like Schumann's *lieder*, Bowles' melodies are heavily dependent on their harmonic support.

Bowles' composing method, as he has described it to me, consisted of making up the music and writing it down when it was done. This is not as commonplace a practice as it may seem to a non-composer. Many, if not most, classically trained composers work back and forth between the keyboard and the written score, outlining a melody and then sketching in an accompaniment, or slowly piecing together a continuity from fragments. It is unusual for a composer to make up a piece in its entirety without notating along the way, and this method has its advantages and disadvantages. At its best, it may produce work in clear-cut short forms that sounds well and feels organically con-
p. 124 structed. On the other hand, it may lead to episodic longer movements and definitely precludes complex contrapuntal structures. Not surprisingly, Bowles' songs exhibit the qualities of clarity, brevity, and sensuousness.

A stickler for the strict observance of a constant tempo in his instrumental music, Bowles allows much more ebb and flow in the tempos of his songs, particularly those of the slow "ballad" type. *The Blue Mountain Ballads* are full of marked tempo changes, and it is likely that similar tempo changes might be implicit in many more of the songs. The recordings on the 1945 album *Night Without Sleep*, presumably made under the supervision of the composer, are full of expressive pauses, *rallentandi, accelerandi* and dynamic nuances which probably are not marked in the unpublished scores. Bowles' notation style is plain and straightforward—nothing but the notes. Some would argue that an intuitive grasp of the musical intention is a *sine qua non*; all the notation in the world can't make a musician play or sing persuasively if he or she does not understand what the music is about. Like many contemporary composers, Bowles has had reason to complain that, in the words of Arnold Schoenberg, "my music isn't modern, it's just poorly performed."

The songs of Paul Bowles are like whiffs of rare and exotic perfumes, richly evocative but evanescent. Many of them make one nostalgic for times and places that have disappeared. Like their author, they are sophisticated p. 125
and charming and wear their learning lightly; in their modest way, the songs cover an enormous range of styles and modes of expression. Although he claims to dislike vocal music, Bowles has made an important contribution to the song literature.

Bohio nativo.
Palm Thatched Home near San Alberto P. R.

THIS SPACE FOR WRITING MESSAGES

Published by González Padín Co. Inc., San Juan-Ponce-Mayaguez, P. R.
Made in Germany.

Dear Miss Stein.
I had no desire to
come to America and
have no idea why I
did now that I am
here. I think it was
my mother! At any
rate, from what I
have been seeing of
Puerto Rico, our coun-
try is stranger than
ever. Best, Freddy
150-10 86 Avenue Jamaica N.Y.

AUTOCHROM

POST CARD

SAN JUAN MAY 6 3:30 PM 1933

AIR MAIL CORREO

UNITED STATES POSTAGE 3 WASHINGTON 3

THIS SPACE FOR ADDRESS ONLY

Miss Gertrude Stein
Bilignin
par Belley
Ain
FRANCE

r A8208

THE RETURN TRIP
(DE VUELTA)

LES SONS RENTRERONT DANS L'ORGUE ET
L'AVENIR S'INVAGINERA DANS LE PASSÉ
COMME IL A TOUJOURS FAIT — H. M.

Imagine a situation involving a man with two lives moving in opposite directions simutaneously, one of which goes toward the future in usual fashion (from today to tomorrow, from childhood to maturity and on to old age), while the other life goes toward the past. Thus, inside the child born in 1910 there lived a man in his eighties. This would explain how in 1930 Gertrude Stein, after exchanging letters, was convinced that her correspondent was a gentleman of at least seventy. So that today we have an octogenarian in whom is imprisoned a child travelling into the past. And this explains how one forgets that he is old, and how being in his company provides a delight similar to that provoked, as if through contagion, by the presence of small children. More than half a century ago those attempting to educate him considered him a stubborn youth; they warned him that unless he studied music as tradition demanded, he would never succeed in being a composer. But they were unware that this student needed no other teacher than himself, because in spite of his youthful appearance he had already made the return trip.

—RODRIGO REY ROSA, TANGIER, 1995

In 1958, Paul Bowles was awarded a grant by the Rockefeller Foundation to travel throughout Morocco to record indigenous music for the Library of Congress. The proposed length of the travel involved was six months; Bowles spent the better part of two years scouring rural communities for authentic music. Bowles' travel companions, to whom he refers in the following excerpts from travel diaries of the second trip (it lasted five and a half months), were Christopher Wanklyn and Mohammed Larbi. In 1972 the Library of Congress issued a two-volume LP record set of a selection of the recordings that are still housed in their Archive of Folk Song under the title Music of Morocco.

THE RIF, TO MUSIC

from **Paul Bowles, THEIR HEADS ARE GREEN AND THEIR HANDS ARE BLUE**

The most important single element in Morocco's folk culture is its music. In a land like this, where almost total illiteracy has been the rule, the production of written literature is of course negligible. On the other hand, like the Negroes of West Africa the Moroccans have a magnificent and highly evolved sense of rhythm which manifests itself in the twin arts of music and the dance. Islam, however, does not look with favor upon any sort of dancing, and thus the art of the dance, while being the natural mode of religious expression of the native population, has not been encouraged here since the arrival of the Moslem conquerors. At the same time, the very illiteracy which through the centuries has precluded the possibility of literature has abetted the development of music; the entire history and mythology of the people is clothed in song. Instrumentalists and singers have come into being in lieu of chroniclers and poets, and even during the most recent chapter in the country's evolution — the war for independence and the setting up of the present pre-democratic regime — each phase of the struggle has been celebrated in countless songs.

The neolithic Berbers have always had their own music, and they still have it. It is a highly percussive art

with complicated juxtapositions of rhythms, limited scalar range (often of no more than three adjacent tones) and a unique manner of vocalizing. Like most Africans, the Berbers developed a music of mass participation, one whose psychological effects were aimed more often than not at causing hypnosis. When the Arabs invaded the land they brought with them music of a very different sort, addressed to the individual, seeking by sensory means to induce a state of philosophical speculativeness. In the middle of Morocco's hostile landscape they built their great walled cities, where they entrenched themselves and from which they sent out soldiers to continue the conquest, southward into the Sudan, northward into Europe. With the importation of large numbers of Negro slaves the urban culture ceased being a purely Arabic one. (The child of a union between a
p. 130 female slave and her master was considered legitimate.) On the central plains and in the foothills of the mountains of the north the Berber music took on many elements of Arabic music; while in the pre-Sahara it borrowed from the Negroes, remaining a hybrid product in both cases. Only in the regions which remained generally inaccessible to non-Berbers — roughly speaking, the mountains themselves and the high plateaux — was Berber music left intact, a purely autochthonous art.

My stint, in attempting to record the music of Morocco, was to capture in the space of the six months which the Rockefeller Foundation allotted to me for the project, examples of every major musical genre to be found within the boundaries of the country. This required the close cooperation of the Moroccan government, everyone agreed. But with which branch of it? No one knew. Because the material was to belong to the archives of the

Library of Congress in Washington, the American Embassy in Rabat agreed to help me in my efforts to locate an official who might be empowered to grant the necessary permission, for I needed a guarantee that I would be allowed to move freely about the untraveled parts of the country, and once in those parts, I needed the power to persuade the local authorities to find the musicians in each tribe and round them up for me.

We approached several ministries, some
of which claimed to be in a position to grant such
permission, but none of which was willing to give
formal approval to the project. Probably there was
no precedent for such an undertaking, and no one
wanted to assume the responsibility of creating such
a precedent. In desperation, working through personal channels, I managed eventually to evolve a
document to which was stapled my photograph,
with official stamps and signatures; this paper made p. 131
it possible to start work. By this time it was early
July. In October, when I had been at work for more
than three months, I received a communication from
the ministry of foreign affairs which informed me
that since my project was ill-timed I would not be
allowed to undertake it. The American Embassy
advised me to continue my work. By December the
Moroccan government had become aware of what
was going on; they informed me summarily that no
recordings could be made in Morocco save by special permission from the Ministry of the Interior. By
then I had practically completed the project, and the
snow was beginning to block the mountain passes,
so this blow was not too bitter. However, from then
on it was no longer possible to make any recordings which required the cooperation of the government; this deprived the collection of certain tribal

musics of southeastern Morocco. But I already had more than two hundred and fifty selections from the rest of the country, as diversified a body of music as one could find in any land west of India.

Christopher [Wanklyn] is a level-headed Canadian with a Volkswagen and all the time in the world. Mohammed Larbi, a good contact man and assistant, as a youth had spent a year accompanying an expedition across the Sahara to Nigeria. The three of us set out together from Tangier following four roughly circular itineraries of five weeks' duration each: southwestern Morocco, northern Morocco, the Atlas, and the pre-Sahara. Between trips we recuperated in Tangier. The pages which follow were written from day to day during the course of the second journey, most of whose days were spent in the mountains of the Rif, in what used to be the Spanish protectorate....

p.132 AUGUST 31, 1959

4 A.M.

The *Caid* of Einzoren proved to be a jolly young man from Rabat, not much more than twenty years old. He is enjoying himself enormously up here in the Rif, he confided, because he has a girl in Einzoren, a "hundred percent Española," named Josefina. In the middle of our recording session he invited us to have dinner with him and Josefina. We accepted, but were given a table where we sat alone eating the food he had ordered for us, while he sat with Josefina and her family.

We had set up the recording equipment in an empty municipal building which stood in the middle of the main plaza. It gave the impression of being a school which was no longer in use. When we arrived, we found one of the rooms already filled with women and girls, three dozen or so of them, singing and tapping lightly on their drums. They sat in straight-backed chairs, their heads and shoulders entirely hidden under the bath towels they wore. A great hushed crowd of men and boys stood outside in the plaza, pressing against the building, trying to peer over the high window sills. Now and then someone whispered; I was grateful for their silence.

The tribe was the Beni Uriaghel, but in spite of that there was no *zamar*. It was a great disappointment. I questioned the *caid* about the possibilities of finding one. He knew even less than I about it; he had never suspected the existence of such an instrument. The musicians themselves shook their heads; the Beni Uriaghel did not use it, they said. Not even in the country, I pursued, outside Einzoren? They laughed, because they were all rustics from the mountains roundabout and had been summoned to the village to take part in the 'festival.'

No one had told me that the girls were going to sing in competitive teams, or that each vil- p. 133
lage would be represented by two rival sets of duo-vocalists, so that I was not prepared for the strange aspect of the room. They sat in pairs, their heads close enough together so that each couple could be wholly covered by the one large turkish towel. The voices were directed floorward through the folds of cloth, and since no gesture, no movement of the head, accompanied the singing, it was literally impossible to know who was performing and who was merely sitting. The song was surprisingly repetitious even for Berber music; nevertheless I was annoyed to have it marred by the constant sound of murmurs and whispers and sotto-voce remarks during the performance, an interference the microphone would inevitably register. But there was no way of catching anyone's eye, since no eyes were visible. Even the matrons, who were supplying the

drumming, were covered. The first selection went on and on, strophe after strophe, the older women tapping the membranes of their disc-shaped *bendirs* almost inaudibly on arbitrary offbeats. I took advantage of the piece's length to leave the controls and go over to whisper a question to the *caid*, who sat beaming in an honorific armchair, flanked by his subordinates who were crouching on the floor around him. "Why are they all talking so much?" I asked him.

He smiled. "They're making up the words they're going to sing next," he told me. I was pleased to hear that the texts were improvised and went back to my Ampex and earphones to wait for the song to end. When the girls had gone on for thirty-five minutes more, and the tape had run out, I tiptoed across the room once again to the *caid*.

"Are all the pieces going to be this long?" I inquired.

p. 134 "Oh, they'll go on until I stop them," he said. "All night, if you like."

"The same song?"

"Oh, yes. It's about me. Do you want them to sing a different one?"

I explained that it was no longer being recorded, and he called a halt. After that I was able to control the length of the selections.

Presently word arrived that the *rhaita* group was sitting in a café somewhere at the edge of town, waiting for transportation; and so, accompanied by a *cicerone*, Christopher drove out to fetch them. The café proved to be in a village about twenty kilometers distant. The men were playing when he arrived; when he told them to get into the car they did so without ceasing to play. They played all the way to Einzoren and walked into the building where I was without ever having interrupted the piece. I let them finish it, and then had them taken back outside into the public square. Mohammed Larbi carried the microphone out and set it up in the middle of the great circle formed by the male onlookers. The *rhaita*, a super-oboe whose jagged, strident sound has been developed precisely for long-distance listening, is not an indoor instrument.

While we were away in the restaurant, the men and the women in the public square somehow got together and put on a *fraja*. This would not have happened in the regions of Morocco where Arab culture has been imposed on the population, but in the Rif it is not considered improper for the two sexes to take part in the same entertainment. Even here the men did not dance; they played, sang and shouted while the women danced. I heard the racket from the restaurant and hurried back to try and tape it, but as soon as they saw what I was doing they became quiet. There was a group of excellent musicians from a village called Tazourakht; their music was both more primitive and more precise rhythmically than that of the others, and I showed open favoritism in asking for more of it. This proved to be not too good an idea, for they were the only men to belong to another tribe, the Beni Bouayache. The recording session, which had been in progress since dusk, gave signs of being about to degenerate into a wild party somewhere around two o'clock in the morning. I suggested to the *caid* that we stop, but he saw no reason for that. At twenty to three we disconnected the machines and packed them up. "We're going on with this until tomorrow," said the *caid*, declining our offer of a ride to Alhucemas. The sounds of revelry were definitely growing louder as we drove away.

August 31

Last night was really enough; we ought to go on eastward. But the governor has gone out of his way to be helpful and has arranged another session in Ismoren, a village in the hills to the west, for tomorrow evening. Today I succeeded in enticing the two Riffian maids at the hotel here into my room to help me identify sixteen pieces on a tape I recorded in 1956. I knew it was all music from the Rif, but I wanted to find out which pieces were from which tribes, in order to have a clearer idea of what each genre was worth in terms of the effort required to capture it. The girls refused to come into the room without a chaperone; they found a thirteen-year-old boy and brought him with them. This was fortunate, because the boy spoke some Moghrebi, while they knew only Tarifcht and a few words of Spanish. I would play a piece and they would listen for a moment before identifying its source. Only two pieces caused them any hesitation, and they soon agreed on those. I still need examples of the Beni Bouifrour, the Beni Touzine, the Ait Ulixxek, the Gzennaia and the Temsaman. The girls were delighted with the small sum I gave them; upon leaving the room they insisted on taking some soiled laundry with them to wash for me.

Nador, September 6

We went up to Ismoren as scheduled, at twilight on the following day. The landscape reminded me of central Mexico. The trail from the highway up to the village was a constant slow climb along a wide, tilting plain. The *caid* was not at home; there had been a misunderstanding and he was in Alhucemas. The villagers invited us into his home, saying that the musicians were ready to play when we wanted to begin. It was a Spanish house with large rooms, dimly lit and sparsely furnished. There were great piles of almonds lying about in the corners; they reached almost up to the ceiling. The dank odor they gave off made the place smell like an abandoned farmhouse. The feeble electricity trembled and wavered. I had Mohammed Larbi test the current because I suspected it of being direct. Unhappily, that was what it proved to be, and I had to announce that in spite of all the preparations it was not going to be possible to record in Ismoren. There was incredulity and then disappointment on all faces. "Stay the night," they told us, "and tomorrow perhaps the electric force will be better." I thanked them and said we could not do that, but Mohammed Larbi, exasperated by their ignorance, launched into an expository monologue about electricity. Nobody listened. Men were beginning to bang drums outside on the terrace, and someone who looked like the local schoolteacher was delegated to serve tea. He invited me to preside at the *caid*'s big desk. When they saw me sitting there, they laughed. An elderly man remarked, "He makes a good *caid*," and they all agreed. I opened three packs of cigarettes and passed them around. Everyone was looking longingly at the equipment, wanting very much to see it set up. We had tea, more tea, and still more tea, and finally got off for Alhucemas to a noisy accompaniment of *benadir*, with two men running ahead of us along the cactus-bordered lanes to show us the way out of the village.

And so each morning I continued to go down to the government offices to study their detailed wall maps and try to locate the tribes with which I hoped to make contact. The first day I had spotted an official surreptitiously looking up our police records; apparently they were satisfactory. The governor and his aides had begun with a maximum of cordiality; but as the novelty of seeing us wore off, their attitude underwent a metamorphosis. It seemed to them that we were being arbitrary and difficult in our insistence upon certain tribes instead of others, and they had had enough of telephoning and making abortive arrangements. It involved about two hours' work for them each day. It was the electricity which frustrated us every time; we had been supplied with a transformer but not with a generator, and Einzoren appeared to be the only village in the region with alternating current....

SEPTEMBER 7

My anxiety was unnecessary. When we got to Segangan this morning, we were taken to a
p. 138 completely different garden, quite outside the town. The *khalifa*'s electrician had already installed the cable, and everything went with beautiful smoothness.

Among the Berbers, not only in the Rif, but much further south in the Grand Atlas, the professional troubadour still exists; the social category allotted him is not exactly that of an accepted member of the community, but neither is he a pariah. As an entertainer he is respected; as an itinerant worker he is naturally open to some suspicion. The Riffians are fond of drawing an analogy between the *imdyazen* (as the minstrels are called both here and in the Atlas) and the *gitanos* of Spain — only, as they point out, the *imdyazen* live in houses like other people and not in camps outside the towns like the gypsies. If you ask them why that is, they will usually reply: "Because they are of the same blood as we." In Segangan I had my first encounter with the *imdyazen*. Their *chikh* looked liked

a well-chosen extra in a pirate film — an enormous, rough, good-natured man with a bandanna around his head instead of a turban. He, at last, had a *zamar* with him. Even Mohammed Larbi had never seen one before. We examined it at some length and photographed it from various angles. It consists of two separate reed pipes wired together, each with its own mouthpiece and perforations; fitted to the end of each reed is a large bull's horn. The instrument can be played with or without the horns, which are easily detached. Yesterday the effusive *khalifa* promised me two *zamar*s, and even this morning he let me go on believing, for the first half-hour or so, that a second player would be forthcoming. But when I began to seem anxious about his arrival and made inquiries among some of the officials, meaningful glances were exchanged, and the language abruptly shifted from Moghrebi into p. 139
Tarifcht. I realized then that I was being boorish; one does not bring a lie out into the open. For some personal reason the *chikh* did not want another *zamar*, and that was that. He was an expert on his instrument, and he played it in every conceivable manner; standing, seated, while dancing, with horns, without, in company with drums and vocal chorus, and as a solo. He insisted on playing it even when I asked him not to. Within two hours my principal problem was to make him stop playing it, because its sound covered that of the other instruments to such an extent that there was a danger of monotony in sonorous effect. I finally seated him ten or twelve yards away from the other musicians. He went on playing, his cheeks puffed out like balloons, sitting all alone under an orange tree, happily unaware that his music was not being recorded.

One very good reason why I wanted to cut out the *zamar* was the presence among the players of an admirable musician named Boujemaa ben Mimoun, one of the few North African instrumentalists I have seen who had an understanding of the concept of personal expression in interpretation. His instrument was the *qsbah*, the long reed flute with the low register, common in the Sahara of southern Algeria but not generally used in most parts of Morocco. I had been trying to get a *qsbah* solo ever since I had found a group of Rhmara musicians in Tetuan. The Rhmara had agreed to do it, but their technique was indifferent and their sound was not at all what I had hoped for. Again I tried at Einzoren, and got good results musically, but once more not in the deep octave, which because of the demands it makes on breath control is the most difficult register to manage.

When I drew ben Mimoun aside and
p.140 asked him if he would be willing to play a solo, he was perplexed. He wanted to please me, but as he said, "How is anybody going to know what the *qsbah* is saying all by itself, unless there is somebody to sing the words?" The *chikh* saw us conferring together and came over to investigate. When he heard my request, he immediately proclaimed that the thing was impossible. Ben Mimoun hastily agreed with him. I continued to record, but clandestinely carried my problem to the *caid* of the village from which the *imdyazen* had been recruited. He was sitting, smoking *kif* with some other notables in a small *pergola* nearby. He seemed to think that a *qsbah* could play alone if it were really necessary. I assured him that it was, that the American government wished it. After a certain length of time spent in discussion, during which Mohammed Larbi passed out

large quantities of *kif* to everyone, the experiment was made. The *chikh* saved face by insisting that two versions of each number be made — one for *qsbah* solo and one with sung text. I was delighted with the results. The solos are among the very best things in the collection. One called "Reh dial Beni Bouhiya" is particularly beautiful. In a landscape of immensity and desolation it is a moving thing to come upon a lone camel driver, sitting beside his fire at night while the camels sleep, and listen for a long time to the querulous, hesitant cadences of the *qsbah*. The music, more than any other I know, most completely expresses the essence of solitude. "Reh dial Beni Bouhiya" is a perfect example of the genre. Ben Mimoun looked unhappy while he played, because there was a tension in the air caused by general disapproval of my procedure. Everyone sat quietly, however, until he had finished.

After that they went back to ensemble playing and dancing. The *kif* had sharpened not only their sense of rhythm but their appetites as well, and I could see that we had come to the end of the session. As the drummers frantically leapt about, nearly tripping over the microphone cable, a tall man in a fat turban approached the microphone and began to shout directly into it. "It's a dedication," explained the *caid*. First there was praise of the Sultan, Mohammed Khamiss, as well as of his two sons, Prince Moulay Hassan and Prince Moulay Abdallah. After that came our friend the Governor of Alhucemas Province (because in the 1958 Riffian war of dissidence he found a solution which pleased nearly everybody), and finally, with the highest enthusiasm, came a glorification of the Algerian fighters who are being slaughtered by the French next door, may Allah help them. (Drums and shouting, and the bulls' horns pointing toward the sky, spouting wild sound.) We drank far too much tea and got back here to Nador too late to eat in the juke box restaurants on stilts, so we opened some baked beans and ate them in the filth and squalor of my room....

September 18

I stayed in bed yesterday morning. About three in the afternoon I got up long enough to drive to the governor's office. He too was in Meknès with the Sultan, and his *katib* was politely uncooperative. His jurisdiction extended to the Beni Snassen, he agreed, but the truth was that the Beni Snassen had absolutely no music; in fact, he declared, they hire their musicians from the Beni Uriaghel when they need music. Nothing. And Figuig? I suggested. "There is no music in Figuig," he said flatly. "You can go. But you will
p. 142 get no music. I guarantee you that." I understood that he meant he would see to it that we got none. The anger was beginning to boil up inside me, and I thought it more prudent to get out of his office quickly. I thanked him and went back to bed. He is not an unusual type, the partially educated young Moroccan for whom material progress has become such an important symbol that he would be willing to sacrifice the religion, culture, happiness, and even the lives of his compatriots in order to achieve even a modicum of it. Few of them are as frank about their convictions as the official in Fez who told me, "I detest all folk music, and particularly ours here in Morocco. It sounds like the noises made by savages. Why should I help you to export a thing which we are trying to destroy? You are looking for tribal music. There are no more tribes. We have dis-

solved them. So the word means nothing. And there never was any tribal music anyway — only noise. *Non, monsieur,* I am not in accord with your project." In reality, the present government's policy is far less extreme than this man's opinion. The music itself has not been much tampered with — only the lyrics, which are now indoctrinated with patriotic sentiments. Practically all large official celebrations are attended by groups of folk musicians from all over the country; their travel and living expenses are paid by the government, and they perform before large audiences. As a result the performing style is becoming slick, and the extended forms are disappearing in favor of truncated versions which are devoid of musical sense.

OUJDA, SEPTEMBER 20

I have lain in bed for the past three days, feverish and depressed, having lost the Beni Snassen as well as the others. Now all that remains open to me in the way of Riffian music is that of the Gzennaia. They live in the Province of Taza, and it will probably be difficult to get to them because of the roads.

During the day there seems to be no sound from the front, but at night the bombardments begin, shortly after dark, and continue for three or four hours. Mohammed Larbi refuses to go out of the hotel; he claims Oujda is a dangerous place these days. According to him, there are ambushes and executions daily. I suspect that most of the explosions we hear during the day are fireworks celebrating the beginning of Mouloud, but I agree that some of the sounds are hard to explain away in that manner. In any case, the city is too close to the border to be restful. All I want is to be well enough to leave for Taza.

TAZA, SEPTEMBER 22

Yesterday morning I had no fever at all, so in spite of feeling a little shaky, I got up and packed, and we set out on the road once more. It was a cool, sunny morning when we left. As we got into the desert beyond El Ayoun, however, the heat waves began to dance on the horizon. We ate in a wheatfield outside Taourirt. Passers-by stopped under the tamarisk trees and sat down to watch us. When we got back into the car there was a struggle going on among several of them for possession of the empty tins and bottles we had left.

By the time we arrived in Taza it was nearly sunset, and I was ready again for bed. But since the government buildings had not yet shut for the night I decided to try and see the governor while I was still up and walking around. I had a feeling that the fever had returned. I went
p. 144
straight to the hotel from there to get into bed, and I have not yet got out of it, so it is just as well that I stayed up an extra hour and saw the *katib*. The governor, not surprisingly, was in Meknès with the Sultan.

This *katib* was a young intellectual with thick-lensed glasses. He made it clear that he thought my project an absurdity, but he did not openly express disapproval. He even went through the motion of telephoning all the way to Aknoul to a subordinate up there in the mountains.

"I see, I see," he said presently. "He died last year. Ah, yes. Too bad. And Tizi Ouzli?" he added, as I gestured and stage-whispered to him. "Nothing there, either. I see." He listened awhile, commenting in monosyllables from time to time, then finally thanked his informant and hung up.

"The last *chikh* in Aknoul died last summer. He was an old man. There is no music in the region. In Tizi

Ouzli the people won't come out. When the Sultan went through, the women refused to leave their houses to sing for him. So you see" — he smiled, spreading his hands out, palms up — "it will not be possible with the Gzennaia."

I sat looking at him while he spoke, already aware of what he was going to report, letting fragments of thoughts flit through my tired head. How they mistrust and fear the Riffians! But how naïve this one is to admit openly that the alienation is so great! Were the women punished? And I remembered a remark a Riffian had once made to me, "You have your Negroes in America, and Morocco has us."

"End of the Rif," I said sadly to Christopher.

The young *katib* pointed to the wall map behind his desk. "In the Middle Atlas, on the other hand, I can arrange something for you. Within a very few days, if you like. The Ait Ouaraine."

"Yes, I should like it very much," I told him.

"Come, please, tomorrow morning at p.145
ten o'clock."

"Thank you," we said.

I came back here to the Hôtel Guillaume Tell and got into bed. The room is not made up here, either, but there is plenty of space in it and my meals are brought up on a tray, so it is not important. Yesterday Christopher and Mohammed Larbi made contact in the street with a group of professional musicians who agreed to record today. Their ensemble consisted of three *rhaita*s, four *tbola* (beaten with sticks) and eight rifles. The first price asked was high; then it was explained that if the rifles were not to be fired during the playing the cost would be cut in half. The agreement reached provided that only the *rhaita*s and *tbola* would perform.

Mohammed Larbi's excessive consumption of *kif* has given him a serious chronic liver disorder; he feels ill most of the time. Last night he went out for a walk after dinner. At the end of an hour he came in, his expression more determined than usual, and announced to us: "I'm finished with *kif*." Christopher laughed derisively. To implement his words, Mohammed Larbi tossed both his *naboula*, bulging with *kif*, and his cherished pipe, on my bed, saying, "Keep all this. You can have it. I don't want to see any of it again." But this morning before breakfast he went out and bought a fifth of Scotch, which he sampled before his morning coffee. When he came into my room later to pack up the recording equipment, he had the bottle with him, and Christopher made loud fun of him.

"O chnou brhitsi?" he cried indignantly. "I'm not smoking *kif* any more. Do you expect me to leave my poor head *empty*?" This amused Christopher and depressed me. I foresee difficulties with a belligerent Mohammed Larbi. *Kif* keeps men quiet and vegetative; alcohol sends them out to break shop windows. In Mohammed Larbi's case it often means a fight with a policeman. I watched with misgivings as he prepared to go out.

This was the first time any recording had been done in my absence. But it all went smoothly, said Christopher on their return. There was a slight altercation at the moment of payment, because in spite of the agreement by which the men were not to discharge their rifles, they had not been able to resist participating, so that at three separate points in the music they fired them off, all eight of them, and simultaneously. At the end they presented a bill for twenty-four cartridges, which Mohammed Larbi, by then well fortified with White Label, steadfastly refused to pay. "All right. Good-bye," they said, and they went happily off to play at a wedding in a nearby village....

Paul I met in 1934 in New York City through Aaron Copland. The Depression was devastating. Paul dressed and looked and smoked as though he were some young American potentate, effete and very blonde and very chichi. I did not like him at first encounter. But — he was the first to publish me in 1935 in his Editions de la Vipère — my Eight Piano Pieces and my First Piano Sonatina, the musical notation which he himself autographed. I was very grateful to him for this although I had to pay him $50 to do so for a certain number of copies. I knew nothing of his literary gifts. I appraised (at my age then of twenty) his musical gifts as minimal and minor, but for the theater, his incidental musical hit the right targets subtly. Some of his songs were vocally affecting but the piano parts rather dull despite some Latin-American influences. As Paul evolved as a writer I read him with much interest. The subject matter did not surprise me. Paul was an American exotic so why not transfer his fantasies to adopted countries and places of sinister inferences? Paul was never sinister, merely irritating in his affectations. We never became close friends but every now and then we would find each other in Rome, on a ship, he crossing over to Africa and I to America. Sixty years later Paul's music is coming forward. May it persevere. As he confronts old age stoically I can only admire his froideur in doing so. (He will like this word I am certain. Paul never liked to be touched, I remember.) In the final phase he may turn out to be the wiser man. And we have remained steadfastly creative. That alone is worthy of a form of friendship hard to define.

David Diamond,

22 April 1995

Bowles Chronology*

(through 1962)

1910

Paul Frederic Bowles is born 30 December, Jamaica, New York

1929

Meets and commences study with Aaron Copland

Attends University of Virginia for two semesters

1930

Aria, Chorale and Rondo (piano solo)

1930/31

Sonata for Oboe and Clarinet

Tamanar (piano solo)

1931

Meets Gertrude Stein and, through her, Virgil Thomson, Paris

1932

Sonata No. I for Flute and Piano

Scènes d'Anabase (based on texts by St. John Perse; 5 songs for tenor, oboe and piano)

1932/33

Sonatina No. I for Piano

1933

Suite for Orchestra (Pastorale, Havanaise, Divertissement)

Cantata 'Par le Detroit' (soprano, four male voices and harmonium)

8, Impasse de Tombouctou (piano solo)

La Femme de Dakar (piano solo)

Guayanilla (piano solo)

Bride of Samoa (film score)

1934

Sonata for Violin and Piano

Innocent Island (film score)

1935

Sonatina No. 2 for Piano

Nocturne (for two pianos)

Fantasia for Two Pianos

Memnon (suite for voice and piano; lyrics by Jean Cocteau)

Venus and Adonis (film score)

*excepting songs, which are too numerous to list here

1936

Trio for Violin, Cello and Piano

Horse Eats Hat (theater music)

Who Fights This Battle? (theater music)

The Tragical History of Dr. Faustus (theater music)

145 W. 21 (film score)

Seeing the World (film score)

1937

Mediodía (Grupo de Danzas Mexicanas) (for flute, clarinet, trumpet, piano and string septet)

Yankee Clipper (ballet; orch.)

America's Disinherited (film score)

1938

Paul Bowles and Jane Auer are married, February, New York

Music for a Farce (for clarinet, trumpet, piano and percussion)

Romantic Suite (for six winds and strings, piano and percussion)

Too Much Johnson (theater music)

Chelsea through the Magnifying Glass (film score)

How to Become a Citizen of the U.S. (film score)

The Sex Life of the Common Film (film score)

1939

Huapango No. I and No. 2 ("El Sol") (piano solo)

Suite (for two pianos)

Denmark Vesey (opera; libretto by Charles-Henri Ford)

Tornado Blues (choral; with piano)

Johnny A. (ballet; piano)

My Heart's in the Highlands (theater music)

Film Made to Music (film score)

1940

Love's Old Sweet Song (theater music)

Twelfth Night (theater music)

Roots in the Earth (film score)

1941

Receives Guggenheim Grant to compose opera

SONATINA FRAGMENTARIA (PIANO SOLO)

DANCE (BALLET; PIANO)

PASTORELA (BALLET; 2 VOICES AND ORCHESTRA)

LIBERTY JONES (THEATER MUSIC)

WATCH ON THE RHINE (THEATER MUSIC)

LOVE LIKE WILDFIRE (THEATER MUSIC)

1942

Accepts position as music reviewer for New York Herald Tribune

1943

Publication of Jane Bowles' Two Serious Ladies

THE WIND REMAINS (ZARZUELA FOR PIANO AND ORCH.; LIBRETTO BASED ON TEXT BY FEDERICO GARCÍA LORCA)

EL BEJUCO (PIANO SOLO)

EL INDIO (PIANO SOLO)

SOUTH PACIFIC (THEATER MUSIC)

'TIS PITY SHE'S A WHORE (THEATER MUSIC)

1944

COLLOQUE SENTIMENTAL (BALLET; ORCH.)

THE GLASS MENAGERIE (THEATER MUSIC)

JACOBOWSKY AND THE COLONEL (THEATER MUSIC)

CONGO (FILM SCORE)

1945

Publication of "The Scorpion" in View

ONDINE (THEATER MUSIC)

1946

Resigns from Herald Tribune

SONATA FOR TWO PIANOS

LA CUELGA (PIANO SOLO; PUBL. 1946)

OROSÍ (PIANO SOLO)

SAYULA (PIANO SOLO; PUBL. 1946)

BLUE MOUNTAIN BALLADS (TEXT BY TENNESSEE WILLIAMS)

CYRANO DE BERGERAC (THEATER MUSIC)

THE DANCER (THEATER MUSIC)

LAND'S END (THEATER MUSIC)

ON WHITMAN AVENUE (THEATER MUSIC)

TWILIGHT BAR (THEATER MUSIC)

1947

Leaves New York; settles in Tangier

Partisan Review publishes "A Distant Episode"

PRELUDE AND DANCE (WINDS, PERCUSSION, DOUBLE BASS AND PIANO)

SIX PRELUDES FOR PIANO (PUBL. 1947)

CARRETERA DE ESTEPONA (PIANO SOLO; PUBL. 1947)

SONATINA FOR PIANO SOLO (PUBL. 1947)

IQUITOS (RETITLED TIERRA MOJADA) (PIANO SOLO)

FOLK PRELUDES FOR PIANO SOLO

DREAMS THAT MONEY CAN BUY (FILM SCORE)

1948

CONCERTO FOR TWO PIANOS, WINDS AND PERCUSSION

SUMMER AND SMOKE (THEATER MUSIC)

1949

Publication of The Sheltering Sky

SONATA FOR TWO PIANOS

1950

THE TEMPEST (THEATER MUSIC)

1952

Publication of Let It Come Down

1953

IN THE SUMMER HOUSE (THEATER MUSIC)

1954

A PICNIC CANTATA (TEXT BY JAMES SCHUYLER)

1955

Publication of The Spider's House

1958

NIGHT WALTZ FOR TWO PIANOS

YERMA (LIBRETTO BASED ON TEXT BY FEDERICO GARCÍA LORCA)

EDWIN BOOTH (THEATER MUSIC)

1959

Receives Rockefeller grant to conduct ethnomusicological research

SWEET BIRD OF YOUTH (THEATER MUSIC)

1962

THE MILK TRAIN DOESN'T STOP HERE ANYMORE (THEATER MUSIC)

Contributors:

JONATHAN SHEFFER is a composer and conductor and the Artistic Director of Eos Music Inc.
PHILLIP RAMEY is an American composer and writer; from 1977 to 1993 he was the annotator and program editor of the New York Philharmonic.
ELI GOTTLIEB is an editor, translator and writer whose first novel, *The Boy Who Went Away*, is forthcoming from St. Martin's Press.
K. ROBERT SCHWARZ is a free-lance music journalist based in New York who is writing his dissertation on the music and music criticism of Paul Bowles.
GENA DAGEL CAPONI is the author of the acclaimed biography *Paul Bowles. Romantic Savage* and editor of *Conversations with Paul Bowles*; Dr. Caponi is the director of American Studies at the University of Texas at San Antonio.
PEGGY GLANVILLE-HICKS (1912-1990), an Australian composer, was a close friend of Bowles'; in *Letters from Morocco* (1952), she set to music texts from Bowles' letters to her.
BEN YARMOLINSKY is a composer of operas, chamber music and songs; he lived in Tangier from 1978 to 1982.

Texts:

IMAGES:

PAUL BOWLES, CA. 1992, PHOTOGRAPH BY PHILLIP RAMEY; (**TITLE PAGE**) PAUL BOWLES, TANGIER 1992 (REVERSED), © VITTORIO SANTORO; DESERT, BY EWING GALLOWAY, NY; PAUL BOWLES AND JONATHAN SHEFFER, TANGIER 1995 © CHERIE NUTTING; PAUL BOWLES, TANGIER 1993, © VITTORIO SANTORO; PAUL BOWLES, 1986 © CHERIE NUTTING; PAUL BOWLES, TANGIER 1994, © VITTORIO SANTORO; PAVEL TCHELITCHEW, EMBRACING COUPLE, PEN AND INK, COURTESY OF JONATHAN SHEFFER; PAUL BOWLES, TANGIER 1992, © VITTORIO SANTORO; SCORPION, BY EWING GALLOWAY, NY; EUGENE BERMAN, STUDY, VIEW OF NEW YORK, PEN AND WASH, THE BALTIMORE MUSEUM OF ART: THE CONE COLLECTION, FORMED BY DR. CLARIBEL CONE AND MISS ETTA CONE OF BALTIMORE, MARYLAND, BMA 1950.12.461; HAND OF PAUL BOWLES, TANGIER 1993 © VITTORIO SANTORO; **PLATE I** PAUL BOWLES, TANGIER 1993 © VITTORIO SANTORO; **PLATE II** MAX ERNST, UNTITLED (FORMERLY L'AVIONNE MEURTRIÈRE [MURDEROUS AIRPLANE]), PHOTOMONTAGE, 1920, THE MENIL COLLECTION, HOUSTON; SPANISH SOLDIER (CÓRDOBA FRONT), ROBERT CAPA/MAGNUM; **PLATE III** CAMELS, BY EWING GALLOWAY, NY; **PLATE IV** FRIEDRICH KIESLER, STAGE DESIGN WITH HAT AND SHOES, PHOTOGRAPH RBK 'S-GRAVENHAGE, TIM KOSTER; **COLOR PLATES** KURT SCHWITTERS, OORLOG, COLLAGE, 1931, COURTESY OF DONALD B. MARRON; KERMIT LOVE, 2 COSTUME DESIGNS FOR THE WIND REMAINS, GRAPHITE AND WATERCOLOR, 1943, COURTESY OF KERMIT LOVE; PAUL BOWLES IN TANGIER, PHOTOGRAPH BY PHILLIP RAMEY; **PLATE V** STEFFI KIESLER, PAUL BOWLES, VIRGIL THOMSON, FRIEDRICH KIESLER AND JANE BOWLES AT F.K.'S PENTHOUSE APARTMENT AT 56 SEVENTH AVENUE, 1940s, PHOTOGRAPH COURTESY OF PHILLIP RAMEY; **PLATE VI** LEONARD BERNSTEIN AND HIS SISTER SHIRLEY IN THE GREEN ROOM, 1950, BY RUTH ORKIN, COURTESY OF THE RUTH ORKIN ESTATE; **PLATE VII** GERTRUDE STEIN, BY MAN RAY, 1926, ADAGP/MAN RAY TRUST, PARIS, © 1995; THEO VAN DOESBURG, EINE KLEINE DADA-SOIRÉE, OFFSET LITHOGRAPH, 1922, STEDELIJK MUSEUM, AMSTERDAM; **PLATE VIII** EUGENE BERMAN, SKETCH FOR A STAGE DESIGN, PEN AND WASH, 1930s, THE BALTIMORE MUSEUM OF ART: GIFT OF DR. ELEANOR P. SPENCER, BMA 1959.149; EUGENE BERMAN, DESIGNS FOR IGOR STRAVINSKY, PEN AND INK, 1972, COURTESY OF MARY E. KAPLAN; **PLATE IX** SALVADOR DALÍ, SET FOR COLLOQUE SENTIMENTALE (1948), COURTESY OF ARCHIVES SOCIÉTÉ DES BAINS DE MER—MONTE CARLO; **PLATE X** VIRGIL THOMSON, PHOTOGRAPH COURTESY OF THE NEW YORK PUBLIC LIBRARY FOR THE PERFORMING ARTS; MARCEL DUCHAMP, AVOIR L'APPRENTI DANS LE SOLEIL (TO HAVE THE APPRENTICE IN THE SUN), PHILADELPHIA MUSEUM OF ART: THE LOUISE AND WALTER ARENSBERG COLLECTION; **PLATE XI** NANCY CUNARD AND TRISTAN TZARA BY MAN RAY, 1924, ADAGP/MAN RAY TRUST, PARIS, © 1995; JACQUES DE GHEYN II, FROM THE MASQUERADE SERIES, ENGRAVING, 1595-96, AMSTERDAM, RIJKSPRENTENKABINET; **PLATE XII** PAUL BOWLES ENTANGLED IN VINES, STILL FROM HANS RICHTER, 8 x 8, 1952, PHOTOGRAPH COURTESY OF MUSEUM OF MODERN ART, NEW YORK; POSTCARD FROM PAUL BOWLES TO GERTRUDE STEIN, THE YALE COLLECTION OF AMERICAN LITERATURE, BEINECKE RARE BOOK AND MANUSCRIPT LIBRARY, YALE UNIVERSITY; PAUL BOWLES, 1930s, PHOTOGRAPH COURTESY OF PHILLIP RAMEY.